Gold Fever

A Coming of Age Adventure

Shawn Pominville

Contents

Chapter 1

The Cave

Asher Mason held the small nugget up to the thin stream of sunlight that gushed through a crack in the mountain. It glinted, sparkled, mesmerized. Suddenly and completely he was struck by a fever. The same fever that has caught hold of those early settlers drawn irresistibly to the Yukon. A fever that boiled in the brains of the Conquistadors and the Aztecs they conquered. A fever that drove Roman emperors, and Egyptian kings, and every other great empire through the ages to advance and dominate. A fever that grabbed and held him like a boa constrictor. A fever that could be thrilling, or disastrous, if history is a predictor of the future.

"This can't be the real thing!" He thought to himself as he snapped out of his gold trance.

Years earlier Asher had found some fool's gold embedded in a small chip of quartz resting in one of the many rock piles behind his house. He had been looking for the perfect size stone to finish his latest "fort" which was really no more than a double-stacked ring of rocks.

Asher had brought his gold streaked chip of quartz to school for his third grade teacher to inspect. Mrs. Algonquin had rotated the quartz in her fingers for not nearly long enough.

She proclaimed without ceremony "Fool's gold. You've found fool's gold my boy."

But this. This was no fool's gold. Asher knew this was the real deal. He had never seen anything like this. And the weight of it. Impossibly heavy for the size. No, this was the real thing.

Asher's excitement was dowsed by the sudden remembrance of how late in the day it was. He held his left wrist to the light. Squinting at the faint gray numerals on his Casio watch he could just make out the numbers; 3:14. He would never be back in time for supper. He had better start thinking up an excuse to give his parents.

It had taken him almost four hours to hike along the river to get to where he stood. He knew he could make it back quicker. There had been much meandering, exploring, and even a little fishing. Asher didn't care too much about fishing but it was the ideal excuse to get beyond his parents' .87 acre of land.

Fishing was fun for about five minutes. After that, without even a nibble, it was time to find something else to do. Asher's fourteen-year-old mind did not have the patience for it. And so, as he often did, he had headed up stream not knowing the adventure this lazy Tuesday morning would set into motion.

Asher took one more awed look at the nugget and then quickly stuffed it in his pocket. He had to go, now. He flipped on the Eveready flashlight with its chromed plastic handle and red cap, wishing he had put in new batteries before he had left.

"There's nothin' heavy duty about these batteries," Asher muttered as he struggled with the muted flashlight beam.

He was actually lucky to have this flashlight with him. He had stuck it in his green nylon fishing bag the last time that he had went bull-heading and was delighted to find that he had not put it back where he had found it. Of course where he found it was on his brother's dresser. His brother would not be delighted. Another creative excuse would be in order to at least soften the yelling about "never putting anything back" and "don't ever touch my stuff." But this tongue lashing was the farthest thing from Asher's mind at this moment.

He dropped the pale spotlight to his freezing and soaked feet that were perched on a smooth rounded stone in the middle of the tiny stream. The soles of his well-worn discount sneakers were just above the ice cold water.

"Why didn't I wear my rubber boots?" Asher asked himself and then answered his own question immediately with "because they would have given me blisters after the first hour of walking in them."

He scanned the immediate water around him, half knowing he would not see another glint of gold, though he hoped to divine another nugget into existence.

"He had to go." The nagging thought swirled in his head again.

He shone the light ahead in the direction of the cramped opening he had wriggled through. A feeling of claustrophobia gripped him as he contemplated the passage out.

He pointed the flashlight beam in the opposite direction up stream into the impossible blackness where it was swallowed completely. It might be fifty feet or two miles to the end of the cavern. The light did not reveal the space, but the echoes of his movements suggested maybe a large cathedral-type space lay ahead.

He drew in a deep breath and exhaled a sigh. The air in the cave hung heavy. It was damp and dank, and had the smell of decay. Not putrid, though it was more intense than rotting leaves. The cave reeked of the feeling it evoked; despair. That sinking feeling of despair that had washed over him as he entered the cave was returning and displacing his gold euphoria.

"Not today..." Asher murmured to himself.

Pivoting on his right foot, he strained to see the next protruding stone downstream that was close enough to hop to. He spotted one and swung his left leg toward it. His left foot landed solidly and his right swung to the next stone. Repeating the motions, he skipped downstream moving with the coordination of a seasoned woodsman. Asher did not think of himself as much of an athlete, but he had logged in endless hours practicing this maneuver, traversing the rugged Adirondack woods that he had grown up in.

He moved over this slippery and stony stream bed with as much agility as anyone could have hoped to. In a few strides the glow of the cave entrance brightened into view. A cool breeze brushed over his face hinting there maybe another outlet that allowed the draft.

A few more strides and Asher was at the jagged split in the side of the mountain that served as the cave's entrance and the stream's exit. He reached down to feel the lump in his front pocket of his stone washed jeans. Satisfied the nugget was secure, he contorted his body to fit the odd shaped opening. He inched his way along in a sort of sideways limbo move.

The opening actually narrowed as he progressed, compressing a slight breeze to more like a wind rushing over his face. It roared in his ears as he pushed through into the daylight. Just as he broke the threshold of the mountain, he thought he heard something; something carried on the fringe of the roaring breeze. Maybe a person, or people, crying out in desperation, but in no discernable words. He shivered as he pushed through the opening and was struck with a nauseous fear in his gut.

"What was that?" He surprised himself with the panic that he heard in his own voice.

He heaved himself out of the teeth of the cave entrance, as it clawed and tore at his clothes. And he was out.

He panted furiously from the effort of his extraction and he felt a panic in his chest. He tried to hold his breath to listen. Nothing. Only an annoyed crow in the distance cawing, cawing. He rolled off to the side of the stream and laid flat on his back, still breathing hard, his feeling of fear and dread dissipating in the sunlight.

He obviously did not hear anything. It must have just been the wind, or his claustrophobic panic, or maybe some lightheadedness from his awkward position. He stood up and shook off the dead leaves that clung to his clothes as he tried to shake off the dreadful, foreboding feeling of the cave. His mind reeled with thoughts of fortune and adventure and peril.

"Time to head home." he said aloud to break the silence of the woods and also to convince himself that it really was time to leave. Asher shoved his hand in his pocket to retrieve the nugget. He grasped it and held his hand out in front of him. He slowly opened his hand to reveal the dime size nugget displayed on his palm. He almost expected it not to be there. But there it was. Heavy, and shiny, and definitely real gold.

Returning it to his front jeans pocket, he checked for any hint of a hole in the pocket lining. Retrieving his fishing bag from the nearby tree branch where he had left it before entering the cave, he swung it around his neck. He grabbed his Zebco fishing pole and gave the closed face reel a turn to snug the line into a bow, making it easier to climb through the brush. One last glance at the cave entrance and he started down the mountain.

Chapter 2

The Swamp

As Asher made his way downstream he caught a glimpse of a bird flying low over the treetops. By its slow, deliberate wing beat Asher knew immediately it was a great blue heron. It was rare to see one of these birds, but he had immediately recognized its distinct way of flying. A blue heron is the only bird in upstate New York that flies with that almost prehistoric looking flight. Like an animal that only conquered flight a few generations ago. He paused to watch it glide down behind some maple trees, likely descending to some unknown swamp. Asher could appreciate the enormity of the bird even at that great distance.

"Huh. Two times in one day," Asher mused to himself. "A good omen maybe."

He checked his watch and continued on, picking his way along the stream. The terrain was thick with alder bushes and August-tall weeds that towered over Asher's head, making it impossible to see more than a few feet ahead of him. He was grateful to have the stream to follow as this area could be as confusing as an autumn corn maze.

Asher jumped from stone to stone to sod clump to stone, crisscrossing the stream. He picked his way under, over and through the thick underbrush making hundreds of unconscious decisions that created the easiest path. He only stopped once in a while to untangle his fishing line when it snagged on a branch.

All the while his mind chattered with gold fever questions. "Was there more gold to be found? When could he get back up to the cave? What is this nugget worth? Does anyone else know about the cave? How could he

explore the cave and keep it a secret?
What *was* that sound as he left the cave?"

"Is there more gold?" That was at the forefront of Asher's thoughts. Finding a cave to explore was the single best thing that had ever happened to him. But gold in that cave? That kind of thing only happened in the movies. He felt for the lump in his pocket as that thought of excited disbelief drifted through his mind.

Asher was suddenly yanked from his thoughts to the task at hand. A monstrous swamp lay before him. This was no small obstacle. Unlike the movies, the foot hills of the Adirondack Mountains do not provide meandering streams through picturesque forests for easy filming. No, rather an Adirondack stream's path is gnarly and twisting, doubling back on itself. It travels through brush and thicket, over rocks, and down into swamps, a thousand yards wide.

He could skirt the edge like he did on the way up, but that would cost him an extra half an hour. As late as it was, the only option would be straight through. Through razor grass and biting, buzzing mosquitos, and stinking muck.

The August drought was the only reason that the crossing would be possible at all. Any other time this swamp would be a huge pond with tufts of swamp grass here and there. The scattered vegetation would try to hint at a shallow bottom that just was not there. There would only be boot robbing muck and waist deep waterholes. Asher, unfortunately, could attest to that.

Cautiously he stepped on to a clump of sod feeling the squish under the soles of his sneakers. He sank a few inches and then, plotted his next step. Asher noticed the heat of the day as he moved out into the open. He baked in the sun as he traveled deeper into the swamp. The smell of the rotting vegetation hung in the air like a nauseating fog. One careful step after the other. Squish, squish, squish…

"Whoa!" Asher yelled as he sank to his knee.
"Now what?" Asher said with exasperation.

He rocked forward trying to free his leg from the grip of the sticky mud, feeling the water soak him to his thigh. He lunged forward and his leg came loose, only to have his whole body fall forward, landing hard on his shoulder. His face was almost completely submerged and the rest of his body was under water or mud.

"This is not good," he thought as he slapped at mosquitos buzzing in his ear.

He struggled, and flopped, and finally righted himself, somehow managing to keep hold of his fishing bag and pole. Asher was drenched, and caked in mud head to toe. This would be yet another thing to explain away to his parents. He scraped some of the thick mud off his pants with his hands and flung it into the air creating a mud spatter spray into the water ahead of his feet. He cupped his hand and swiped at the mud on his thigh. As he went to fling the muck off his fingers he suddenly realized there was no lump where there should have been one.

"Where's the nugget?" he said aloud in a high-pitched panicked voice.

Asher frantically wiped his hand off on his jeans and tried to jam it in his pocket. With some effort, he finally wriggled his fingertips in a little way, only to be blocked by the folded up lining of his pocket. He desperately patted down his jeans up by the waistband and finally felt the flattened marble shape that he was sure he had lost. He exhaled a sigh of relief. As he worked to get his pocket lining back into place, he contemplated his next move.

Asher was about half way across the swamp and daylight was dwindling. Surveying the terrain ahead, he made out the remnants of a beaver dam. It was no more than a slightly higher ridge that ran in a large arc across the swamp. The old mound of intertwined sticks and mud would allow for much easier travel even though it was not exactly in the direction Asher needed to go. He trudged toward it, realizing it was his best option.

Soon he was standing on the old beaver berm and much more solid footing. He made his way along the old beaver dam to the edge of the swamp. Asher traversed the last couple hundred yards up on high ground skirting the muck until he once again rejoined the stream. He was hot and wet and stunk of rotting beaver swale. The trip back was not going at all like he would have hoped.

Leaving the swamp for drier ground, Asher was finally making good time. He skipped across stones and downed trees, feeling pretty good about his progress. His mud caked clothes were drying in the August heat. His mind drifted to the mornings journey up stream.

Chapter 3

Uncle Jeb

Asher started his trek this morning on his great uncle's land that is located just behind Asher's house. Asher could climb through the barbwire fence that bordered his yard and in five minutes be fishing on Old Indian Creek. Asher's family had always suspected that his Great Uncle Jeb was part Iroquois Indian, and so the irony of the stream's name was not lost to Asher.

Great Uncle Jeb certainly looked the part. His face was weathered and creased like chewed rawhide. He was tanned dark and red. His high cheekbones offset his ridge bumped nose that flared a little when he spoke of days gone by. He had straight raven black hair bobbed off at the shoulder that he kept crammed in an old green felt hat with a wide brim. He smelled of pipe tobacco, and leather, and history.

These days Great Uncle Jeb could be found sitting on the porch of his ancient hunting cabin that now also served as his home. He rocked ceaselessly in his rocking chair that was older than he was, and likely older than his third generation hunting cabin.

The old Mason family rocking chair creaked on the rock back, but curiously, not the rock forward. This created a disturbing sound, like a grandfather clock that ticked but did not toc. When Asher visited, the unsettling creak…creak… creak… would leave him hoping Uncle Jeb would launch into one of his old timey stories that would stop the rocking for a bit.

This morning was no different than any other. Uncle Jeb was up on his porch rocking and smoking his corn cob pipe as Asher approached. The hunting cabin was situated on the east side of the stream, only a twenty-minute walk from Asher's house. It was so near the stream bank that you could easily cast a line in from the porch. So, heading upstream meant that you were checking in with Great Uncle Jeb.

It actually took longer to drive to Uncle Jeb's place than to walk cross lots. The rough back road to the shack was only a seasonal use highway that ended in a clearing behind the cabin. It was a unbelievably rough drive to the ancient cabin in the woods.

"Hi Uncle Jeb," Asher chimed as he approached the porch.

Uncle Jeb smiled an almost toothless smile at the appearance of Asher. Most any event that strayed from the everyday monotony of the porch sitting was a welcome development in Uncle Jeb's life.

"Doing a little fishin' today?" Uncle Jeb asked in his raspy voice as he eyed Asher's fishing pole.

"A little," Asher answered candidly.

Uncle Jeb offered Asher a grape soda as a means to get Asher to stay a bit longer rather than to keep walking through.

"Sure, Uncle Jeb," Asher agreed as he climbed the rickety stairs to the decaying porch.

"Anything new?" Uncle Jeb inquired knowing what Asher's standard answer would be.

"Nah," Asher replied without giving his answer any thought.

"It's gonna be a hot one," Uncle Jeb predicted as he handed Asher the cold grape soda from the antique refrigerator beside him on the porch.

"Yah. It's pretty hot already," Asher observed as he popped the tab off his aluminum soda can.

Asher bent the soda can tab around another tab that was connected to a hundred more. This created one more link in a seemingly endless chain that hung from the wobbly porch railing. This little ritual was carried out every time Asher stopped to see Uncle Jeb and it put a little smile on Asher's face. He liked the idea of adding to that chain that who knows who started and who knows how long ago.

"The trout will be biting today up past where the creek splits I bet." Uncle Jeb offered as he resumed his rock.

Creak… creak… creak…

"The creek splits?" puzzled Asher.

"I've never seen where it splits," Asher said as he searched his memory of past excursions.

"Yup. You just never been far 'nough up," Uncle Jeb explained.

"If you do try to get up there today, make sure you take the east branch. That's where the fish are," Uncle Jeb advised.

Creak… creak… creak… "Don't take the west branch." Uncle Jeb added with a slightly warning tone.

Asher snapped his head up to look at Uncle Jeb when he had realized he was being cautioned. Uncle Jeb's eyes squinted and his nostrils flared a little revealing to Asher he was lost for the moment in times gone buy.

"Why not the west branch?" Asher asked, suddenly interested in what Uncle Jeb had to say.

"The west branch is bad luck," Uncle Jeb advised.

"My daddy never fished the west branch, I've never fished the west branch, and you shouldn't either." Uncle Jeb said with a gruff in his voice Asher had never heard.

"Never?" Asher ventured.

"Nope. Never," Uncle Jeb said with a finality Asher knew not to pursue.

"Well I think I'm gonna try to make it up to where it splits today then. I'd like to try that east branch," Asher said reassuringly.

"Yup. The east branch. A lot of fish up there," Uncle Jeb said with satisfaction and smirked with his three tooth smirk. Creak... creak...creak...

And with that Asher had left Uncle Jeb's cabin. He had not been able to wait to find the split in the stream and explore the forbidden west branch. And boy, did that defiant decision pay off, so far. Of course Asher was not home yet, not by a long shot.

Chapter 4

The Barker Brothers

Before Asher could reach Uncle Jeb's cabin there was an acre of land that he needed to cross and he dreaded it as he approached. An acre is 202 feet wide by 202 feet long. Old Indian Creek passed through a disputed acre's width of land that the Barker family thought they owned. The problem was that even though it was only 200 feet wide, the 20-acre strip of land was almost a mile long, making it almost impossible to go around it. Uncle Jeb had told Asher that the Barker family does not own that land and never would.

"My family's been payin' taxes on that land for 150 years," Uncle Jeb had railed.

Paying taxes or not, there was Barker posted signs every ten feet along the borders of what the Barker brothers believed to be theirs. Asher had been warned more than once about trespassing on the Barker's land. The last time he got caught crossing the disputed Barker land, Billy Barker had done a lot of yelling at Asher, but Asher did not really care if he got yelled at by Billy. What Asher *did* care about was the rifle Billy Barker had cradled in his arms as he spouted off to Asher.

Asher reached the top of the ridge and dropped flat on his belly. He could smell the summer baked dead pine needles that were inches from his face, their aroma mixing with the remanence of the swamp odor that still clung to him along with his own sweat. He pulled himself forward along the ground, coming to rest at the base of a monstrous pine tree. He craned his head to the side, peering around the trunk of the tree and down to the gully below. Directly in front of him, down in the gully, were the bright orange posted signs lined up like a row of no-parking signs.

Asher waited for the heat bug to quit singing his high pitch hum of praise for the warmth of summer, then held his breath. He heard a red squirrel chatter to express his annoyance with Asher so close to his tree, but that was all. Asher wiped the beads of sweat off his forehead with his shoulder, trying to keep the salty sweat out of his eyes. He scanned the woods that lie within the borders of the disputed Barker land. It was as deserted as a December graveyard.

"It's now or never," Asher whispered to himself.

Asher sprung up from his hiding spot, with heart pounding and chest tight, plunged down the hill towards the stream's edge as fast as his legs would carry him. He managed huge strides as gravity pulled him down the hill. He barely kept upright as he descended. Three, four, five strides and Asher tore past the posted sign barricade. His vision tunneled, as he plotted and executed his course through the brush and over the rocks.

Three more seconds and he would be across the second line of posted signs. Just then his right arm was jerked back hard, wrenching it behind him, causing a shooting pain in shoulder.

"Ouch!" Asher cried out.

The force of it stopped him cold and almost flung him onto his back. His fishing pole line caught on a spruce tree sapling. Asher had his fingers wrapped tightly behind the reel of the pole so it did not allow his hand to slip free when the pole snagged. He glanced back at the snagged line and then up to the orange plastic posted sign nailed to a spindly hemlock just feet ahead of him.

He gave it a hard yank and it snapped free. Simultaneously, Asher heard an echoing crack in the distance.

"A gun shot?" No sooner did that question cross his mind and he could hear a Barker brother yelling obscenities that Asher thought it was just as well he couldn't quite make out.

"Is he really shooting at me?" Asher croaked out loud in an I-can't-believe it voice.

Asher did not want to know the answer to that question and was not sticking around to find out. He tore up the hill, past the signs and kept on running, not even pausing to look over his shoulder. With adrenaline surging, he ran and ran, outpacing whichever Barker brother it was, until the cursing had all but faded away.

Asher's heart pounded in his head and sweat stung his eyes. He leaped up then over a huge downed pine tree and collapsed behind it. He was breathing so hard he thought he was going to hyperventilate. Asher tried to catch his breath as he lay on his back motionless almost under the massive fallen tree. One puffy cloud broke up the blue bowl overhead and he watched it drift for a moment. The sunlight was casting long shadows around him causing Asher to suddenly feel smaller in the bigness of the woods.

He rolled to his side to look between the still attached broken branches that held the pine tree off the ground like legs of a short stool. He tried to hold his breath while he scanned the trees and underbrush, peering in the direction that he had just ran from. Nothing. Not a sound except the swishing of the breeze through the tops of the white pines.

Uncle Jeb's cabin was only a little way now. Asher decided that the coast was clear and slowly rose from his hiding place. He headed back to Old Indian Creek with a slow determination, feeling spent from the ordeal. Down, down, downstream he trekked toward Uncle Jeb and home.

The sun now was almost below the tree line casting even longer shadows on Asher's path indicating it was entirely too late. Finally, Uncle Jeb's cabin came into view and Asher sighed with relief. Not only did this mean he was almost home but also that the Barker brothers would not be an issue any longer.

As crazy as the Barkers were, they would not dare approach Uncle Jeb's place. The loaded shotgun on the porch within arm's reach of the rocking chair was quite a deterrent taking into account Uncle Jeb's willingness to blast away at any target that he deemed worthy. Uncle Jeb's eyesight was terrible which really made him even more dangerous with his shotgun.

Asher approached Uncle Jeb's cabin with a determined walk, his eyes were fixed on his uncle rocking on the ancient cabin porch.

Uncle Jeb called out to him. "It's pretty late Asher. You must've made it to the east branch today. Any luck?"

"Not really," Asher replied candidly as he maintained his march toward home. "Did you see anythin' of those Barker brothers today?" Uncle Jeb bristled with disgust.

Asher didn't want to stir up any more trouble today so he replied with a "Nah, not today."

Asher kept his head down pretending to concentrate on the terrain ahead of him, not wanting Uncle Jeb see his face as he told the lie. For a man that couldn't hardly see, Uncle Jeb seemed to be able to read a face like a book.

"Good," Uncle Jeb said with a nod, squinting his eyes a little. "They know better," he added confidently.

"If only," Asher thought to himself.

"Yah. I'm late for supper. I gotta get goin', Uncle Jeb," Asher explained as he resumed his march past the cabin toward home.

"Tell everybody I said hey," Uncle Jeb offered with a drawn out drawl.

His nostrils flared a little. Creak… creak… creak… The unsettling racket of the rocking chair faded behind Asher as he trudged toward home.

Chapter 5

The Plan

Asher's pace quickened to a jog as he broke the tree line and started through the field. He finally could see the row of fence posts that marked his parent's property line standing like sentries guarding his house. Asher dropped to a walk and stopped at the fence.

He tossed his fishing bag and pole over the fence onto the lawn. He pushed the middle strand of barbwire down and he crawled through. The rusty barbed wire spanning the grey cedar posts hung with too much slack and Asher wondered how it kept their steer in as he stepped through onto his side lawn. The crisp evening air blended the smell of the cedar hedges and the aroma of awaiting dinner to create a welcomed familiar scent. The scent of home.

Asher's family was just finishing supper when he pushed through the back door shouting "I'm home!"

Asher's older brother, Alex and younger sister, Molly was seated at the kitchen table opposite his mother.

"Where have you been?" Asher's mother said with worried annoyance. "We waited almost an hour before we finally sat down to eat."

Asher knew that he was not the only reason supper was held up. His father was working overtime again and his mother had put off supper hoping his father would be home in time.

"I tried a new fishing hole Uncle Jeb told me about. It's way upstream. It took a long time to get there and I fell in the swamp on the way back," Asher explained quickly trying to stick to as close to the truth as possible.

"I got soaked," he added, trying to express exasperation.

His mother frowned and the crease between her eyebrows deepened.

"I was gettin' really worried. You said you would be home for supper," she said with disapproval.

"If this happens again you're not gonna be allowed to go fishin' anymore," she warned as she narrowed her eyes at him. "Now go wash up for supper, and take those muddy sneakers off," she directed.

"I'm sorry, Mom. It won't happen again," Asher offered with as much sincerity as he could muster. As he said this he wondered how he would ever get back to the cave.

Asher washed up and took his seat by his mother at the table. He and his family always sat in the same spot for meals. How and when this seating arrangement was decided, Asher didn't know, but it was alright with him. His father sat at the head of the table, his mother to his right, and Alex and Molly opposite him. So Asher did not sit next to a sibling and that was for the best.

Maybe it was his age or being the middle child, but he did not really get along with his brother and sister. He loved them for sure, but was not able to be around them for any length of time. It always ended in picking at each other. Asher's discovery would not be shared with either one of them. It would not be shared with anyone. It would be his secret.

As Asher pushed his green beans around his plate he turned over the day's events in his head. He needed a plan to get back to that cave and explore it. The trip there and back took up a whole day. He needed be able to stay overnight once he reached the cave but his parents would never agree to an overnight camping trip by himself. How could he make this happen?

Asher's mother told him to hurry and finish up so they could pick up the supper dishes. As he shoveled in the remainder of his supper, an idea began to take shape in his head. He knew his parents would have no problem with him staying with Uncle Jeb for a couple of nights. He had stayed with Uncle Jeb last summer for almost a week to help him do some repairs on the cabin. Asher would convince his parents that he was staying with Uncle Jeb and then tell Uncle Jeb that he was going camping upstream on a fishing trip.

"That might just work," Asher pondered to himself.

He quickly got up from the table to retreat to his bedroom.

"Hold on Asher, bring your plate over to the counter and help pick up," his mother instructed impatiently. "Since when do we just get up from the supper table and leave the mess?"

"Oh, right, sorry," Asher apologized barely hearing his mother as he tried to work out the details of his plan in his head. He helped clean up the supper mess and then headed to the basement.

That is where his bedroom was. It was kind of damp in the summer and cool in the winter but it was private. He did not have to share it with Alex and it was sort of secluded from the rest of the one story house. Asher was so excited when his father had offered to build him his own bedroom in the basement. He had hated sharing a room with his brother.

Alone in his bedroom he sat at a desk his dad had built, perched on a folding chair in front of a blank notebook page.

"Okay, I'm going to need some camping supplies for this plan," Asher contemplated to himself.

He began to make a list:
1. Tent
2. Sleeping bag
3. Flashlight
4. Food
5. Canteen
6. Matches
7. Compass

8. Rope
9. Jackknife

"Something to dig with probably," Asher reasoned. He now thought about an old western he had watched and the gold prospectors in that movie had a pan to somehow sift the gold out of the river. It suddenly dawned on Asher that he knew nothing about gold mining.

"Time to read up on gold mining," Asher announced to himself.

Asher opened the door to his bedroom and walked around to the other end of the basement where a huge stack of drawers stood. The drawers held all kinds of miscellaneous junk. But in the third drawer from the floor, there was a complete set of encyclopedias.

The ancient set of encyclopedias were grossly out of date and had a few missing pages but much of the information in them was still relevant knowledge. Asher ran his fingers along the exposed spines of the antiquated books that were lined up in two neat rows in a huge drawer.

"E" "F" "H" he murmured to himself the order of the volumes.

"Of course they're not in order," Asher said annoyed. "L" "M" "G".

He yanked the volume out and starting thumbing through the pages. A familiar musty smell wafted from the book reminding him of past school projects, sitting at his grandpa's kitchen table, surrounded by snacks set out for him. The encyclopedias originally came from Asher's grandpa's place and then were given to Asher when his grandpa died two years ago. Asher's father said that Asher might as well have them because he was the only one that ever looked at them anyways.

Asher skimmed over *"History of Gold"* and got right to the important part, *"Methods of Mining."* He was going to need a shovel, pick axe. and a large shallow pan with outward sloping sides. The encyclopedia explained that by swirling around the dirt mixed with water, the lighter material would wash over the lip of the pan leaving the much heavier gold in the bottom. Asher had seen this done in movies he had watched without ever really understanding the principle behind it.

Asher returned to his bedroom still reading the article as he sat on his bed. At the end of the article, almost as a footnote, it mentioned New York State specifically and that caught Asher's attention.

It explained that unlike the other states, if someone finds gold or silver in New York State, it was the property of the state, regardless of where it was found. Meaning even if someone finds it in their own back yard it is still the property of New York state. Asher reread the statement to make sure he understood it correctly then sat for a minute to let it sink in.

"That's not right!" That's my Uncle Jeb's land I found it on." He fumed to himself.

"Well, I guess that means that I'm not tellin' anybody about this," he said with resolve.

"Whatever gold I find I'll somehow cut Uncle Jeb in fifty-fifty without him knowin' the details." Asher reasoned to himself.

That was something Asher would have to work out if and when he found more gold. No one would ever find out about any gold that Asher might find, especially New York State.

He ran through his list again adding the mining equipment. He had everything he needed except that pan and some food. Tomorrow was his day to work at the little general store in town. E. B. Marley Co. had been selling everything from flour, to seed potatoes to shovels to shoes and a thousand other things for the last 150 years.

Asher had to get working papers to be able to work there this summer because he wasn't sixteen yet. He was at first a little apprehensive about taking the job, but now he was very glad that he had. Not only did he love to work there, he now would be able to fund and outfit his adventure up to the cave.

"When I go to the store tomorrow I'll find something for a gold pan and get some groceries for the trip," Asher thought to himself as he became excited about his plan taking shape.

Asher pulled the gold nugget out of his pocket to gaze at it once again. He held it close to the chrome plated three bulb light next to his mirror and watched it shimmer in the artificial light. Asher put the nugget between his canine teeth and bit down until he felt his tooth leave a slight depression in the gold. The encyclopedia had said that this was what the old miners would do to determine if the gold was real or not. Gold is a soft enough metal that you can dent it with a bite.

"Yup. The real thing," Asher said aloud with a satisfied grin.

He wrapped the nugget in a Kleenex and placed it in a small white box that he had found in his junk drawer. He knelt down in front of the hiding spot he had created for stuff he didn't want his sibling playing with.

It was a small louvered hot air register that Asher had rigged to swing open rather than be screwed tight to the wall. He had attached hinges to the underside of the register and a magnet to hold it closed. He had replaced the screws by gluing in shorter ones giving the appearance that it was still screwed into place. Asher swung open his makeshift wall safe and carefully placed the little white box inside. Time for bed.

Chapter 6

Claudie

Putting in a restless night Asher was up early the next morning beaming with anticipation for the day to come. He decided to ride his bike to work rather than get a ride from his father. He needed an excuse to take his backpack along so he could bring home his camping supplies undetected. Asher mounted his new red Spalding twelve speed road bike and raced out of his driveway towards town. He had just bought this bike using some of his money he had earned this summer and he loved riding it.

It was a six mile ride to town and Asher pedaled hard along the country road arriving 20 minutes before opening time. He whipped the bike into the pothole filled driveway that ran the length of the old store and parked it next to the back door. He lifted a corner of the ragged rubber door mat to reveal a tarnished brass skeleton key that fit the antique lock of the store's back door. The key was left there so Asher could open up for business without waiting for old man Marley to show up from his house next door.

Asher slipped the key in the old lock and wiggled it as he tried to turn it. With a slight "clunk", the key turned and the lock's bolt slid back into the door. He pushed hard against the brass handle while leaning his shoulder into the upper wood frame of the door. The doors multiple paint layers broke free from the door jamb with a "humph" and the door popped open. Asher replaced the key and stepped inside the store.

He immediately turned right into a little nook nestled in the corner of the back of the building that served as sort of an office. The office space was still open enough so anyone working at the desk could keep an eye on the store.

In the corner of the office space was a gigantic safe set on a concrete slab that was supported by the foundation of the building. The thinking was that if there was a fire the safe would fall out of the building rather than tumble to the basement where it would cook the contents like an oven. Asher retrieved the key for the inner metal door of the safe that was kept in the top desk drawer.

The massive outer safe door had a combination lock that was kept set so it could be opened without twisting the dial. Asher moved the safe's chrome door handle one half turn to the left and gave it a yank. It swung open heavily on the massive chromed hinges. He slid the key into the inner door's lock that was now exposed and unlocked it. This is where the cash drawer for the cash register was kept, complete with the cash and coins already in it, poised to make change for the sales of the day. Asher collected the drawer and walked it up to the antique mechanical cash register that was likely older than he was. He slid the inner change drawer into the old machine and closed it.

His next move should have been unlocking the front doors and moving the wheelbarrows, rakes, shovels, and ladders out to the front of store for display, but Asher wanted to do some shopping of his own before the first customers arrived.

"What can I use for a gold pan?" Asher wondered to himself as he browsed the kitchenware aisle.

He picked up a shallow aluminum pan but decided the sides were too straight and returned it to the shelf. He continued down the aisle until he came to the graniteware. He picked up a blue ceramic coated metal pan that was speckled with white. This pan looked like the one in the encyclopedia and like the ones he had seen on T.V.

"This'll work," he said to himself with satisfaction. "Now I need some food."

He perused the groceries, not really knowing what he should take with him. After much back and forth he finally decided on ten Snickers bars and two bags of Doritos. He reasoned this food would be easy to pack and required no preparation. Not to mention Asher loved this junk food and might as well indulge as long as he was paying for it.

He piled everything on the counter along with a four pack of size C Energizer batteries as he prepared to cash himself out. He glanced at his watch and realized it was five minutes past opening time.

"Shoot," he said with frustration under his breath.

He made for the front doors and unlocked them. As he swung the street doors out toward the sidewalk to be braced open by a bucket of driveway sealer, Asher was greeted by Claudie Buckman.

"Not now," Asher thought to himself with exasperation.

Claudie was that quirky person that wandered Main Street all day, every day. He was that offbeat character it seemed that you could find in almost every small town. With red wagon in tow, Claudie pedaled his adult three wheeled trike up and down Main Street stopping to visit with pedestrians, and shopkeepers, and children, and dogs, and the occasional lamp post.

Claudie lived in an old run down house on the edge of town that had been bequeathed to him from his mother. They claimed he had lived there as a recluse for almost thirty years. Then one day he just showed up on Main Street with his red wagon. He has patrolled Main Street ever since.

Some say that he is bipolar and others say he is just plain crazy, but Asher did not mind him. Claudie stopped into E. B. Marley & Co. pretty much every day and Asher was mostly amused by him. But today Asher wanted to cash himself out and get his camping supplies packed into his backpack before Old Man Marley showed up. He did not have time for Claudie's nonsense.

"How goes it today, Asher?" Claudie asked with a huge grin almost too big for his face as he parked his trike two feet from the front door.

Claudie removed his orange winter wool hat that he wore year round to reveal his practically bald head. The low slant of the early morning August sun reflected off Claudie's shiny head and accented the deep creases in his face.

Asher was not very tall, only about five six, but he towered over Claudie. Standing at just under five feet, Claudie looked even shorter because of the oversized jeans he wore that were way too long for him. Claudie kept the pant legs rolled up along with the sleeves of the camo sweatshirt that he seemed to wear every day regardless of the weather.

"Pretty good, Claudie," Asher answered, trying to hide his annoyance.

As Asher finished propping open the doors, Claudie rummaged through his red wagon. The wagon had side racks on it and was piled to overflowing with Claudie's treasures that he had collected in his travels on Main Street. It was mostly bits of trash; a slip of shiny wrapping paper, various soda and beer cans, half of a wooden crate, some wire clothes hangers, and a hundred other things. An odor, not unlike a compost pile, wafted from the wagon as Claudie stirred up the contents. Asher just hoped that Claudie was not searching for a gift for him.

Claudie finally popped up from his stoop holding a tin can that had long since lost its label.

"Breakfast," he proclaimed triumphantly.

He pulled a too soft Saltine cracker out of the shiny can. Asher could see another piece of mushy cracker and a few other things he could not identify tumbling about in the tin can. Asher declined when Claudie offered him some breakfast.

"How many days had Claudie stored that can in the bottom of his wagon?" Asher pondered to himself.

He learned to politely decline any food that Claudie offered him. One time Asher had seen him drink a half of quart of milk that was completely spoiled judging by the smell and the chunks floating in it. Claudie drank it down happily, apparently possessing a stainless steel stomach.

Asher turned to go back into the store with Claudie on his heels. Claudie had his tin can in one hand and a shiny, sort of broke, pinwheel in the other. The pinwheel was likely his latest find.

Asher slipped behind the solid oak counter and began ringing up his items. There was an old fashioned "cha-ching" with each item entered. You could hear the chatter of the old cash register's worn gears as they grudgingly added up yet another sale for the millionth time.

Claudie stood on the other side of the heavy oak counter watching Asher with a wide grin. People complained about Claudie but they could not say that he was a grump. The guy always wore a grin and seemed to always be happy too. Asher glanced up at him with his pinwheel and tin can and mused how elf-like he looked.

"Going campin', huh?" Claudie speculated.

"Why would you think that?" Asher answered nervously.

"How could he tell I'm going camping from this stuff?" Asher asked himself.

"That looks like campin' stuff to me," Claudie said with a slight rise in his voice. "Where ya goin'?"

Asher thought for a moment and then decided it wouldn't do any harm telling Claudie about camping along Old Indian Creek. He would tell him he was going to camp overnight so he could fish way upstream. Besides, nobody payed attention to what Claudie said anyways.

"Ya. I'm goin' for a couple of days up on Old Indian Creek fishin'," Asher finally answered.

"Did ya know I used to work for your great Uncle Jeb's father, Ansylum Mason, up in those parts?" Claudie asked, still grinning ear to ear.

"You did?" Asher questioned with genuine surprise.

"Just how old was Claudie?" Asher thought to himself.

"Yup. We logged it up there. Well, that is, until Ansylum died in the accident," Claudie said with not enough emotion in his voice.

"After that, well, nobody did much of anything up in that neck of the woods." Claudie explained and his grin lessened to a sort of grimace.

Asher completely stopped what he was doing and looked intently at Claudie.

"What accident?" Asher asked with blazing curiosity, finding it hard to believe Claudie knew anything about the Mason family history.

"Well, me and Ansylum was loggin' up on the west branch of Indian Creek when Ansylum fell a big old white pine that landed in the water. When he waded in to limb up the tree, he noticed somethin' shinin' by his feet. He reached down in the water and picked up a gold nugget."

"A gold nugget?" Asher asked with almost uncontained excitement.

"Yup. You can imagine that we switched from loggin' to lookin' for gold mighty quick. We looked for gold all up and down that creek and found a few more nuggets and panned some dust. When we came on to the head of the creek, we found even more gold. Ansylum saw that the creek was comin' out of a crack in the mountain that looked like it could be a sort of cave. But we couldn't fit through the crack to check it out."

Asher tried to hide his excitement and familiarity with the story Claudie was telling him but his widened eyes and his growing smirk likely betrayed him.

"Oh... Really?" Asher tried to say nonchalantly.

"Well, Ansylum figured there could be a lot more gold in that cave, so we searched for another way in. And we found it," Claudie said with accomplishment.

"You did?" "Where?" Asher asked, dropping any act of nonchalant that he may have been trying to portray.

"Oh, it was about three hundred yards north east and up a ways from the head of the creek," Claudie explained with a grin. He was enjoying the fact Asher was showing such an interest in his story.

"Did you find any more gold in the cave?" Asher asked.

"Well we didn't have a lantern with us and it was late in the day. So we decided to head home, plannin' to go back on Monday to have a look inside. It was Saturday afternoon and nobody worked on Sunday... But I guess Ansylum couldn't wait that long to see what was in that cave."

"He went to check it out on his own?" Asher speculated.

"Not by himself. Him and Jeb. They hiked up there early Sunday morning with a lantern, a pick axe, and a long rope. Ansylum's plan was to go down in the cave to have a look with the lantern and leave Jeb out by the entrance. Jeb would hold the end of the rope that was wrapped around a big cherry tree and Ansylum would tie the other end around his waist. Asylum figured that way he wouldn't get lost or fall if he came to any drop-offs."

"So what did they find?" Asher asked with uncontained excitement.

"Well, I'm gettin' to that. Ansylum was in the cave for a couple of hours before he finally came out to tell Jeb what he found. He told Jeb that way down in a narrow shaft he found a gold vein six inches wide that stretched to where he hadn't found the end to it yet. Jeb told me that his daddy had a look in his eye like he had never seen before when he came out of that cave. Ansylum grabbed the pick axe and headed back into the cave, leaving Jeb to man the rope. Jeb could hear his daddy chipping away somewhere deep in the cave for hours."

"How much gold did they get that day?"

Claudie's face dropped to a frown as he answered Asher's innocent question.

"None," Claudie said flatly.

"Ansylum never came back out. It couldn't have been an earthquake because nobody else felt any tremors that day," Claudie explained.

"Jeb said he heard a huge, low rumble, and then rocks and dirt poured down in front of him."

Asher's face twisted in disbelief.

"The cave entrance was gone and a rock the size of a house laid on the rope Jeb was holdin'. His daddy was gone. Just like that." Claudie said this in a lower tone as he shook his head a little.

"Didn't they try to dig him out?" Asher asked with exasperation.

"Well, there was no heavy equipment around in those days. Jeb yelled and yelled and yelled for his daddy but he never heard another sound from the cave. Jeb was just a boy at the time. Not much older than you. He didn't know what to do. He finally decided to run back home to get help. It took him two hours to get home. By the time some men were rounded up and they made it back to the cave-in, it was almost dark. There were seventeen guys in all, me included. We dug all night and all the next day."

"You never found him," Asher quietly asked with a knowing shake of his head.

"No. We only made it about fifty feet into the mountain. It was mostly great big granite rocks. There was just no way he was still alive. That cave turned into Ansylum's tomb. When we decided that we had done all we could, we all stood at the cave entrance and said our goodbyes and a little prayer. That's the last time I was up there. As a matter of fact, it's the last time anybody I know has been up there."

"I knew that great, great grandpa Ansylum died young, but I've never heard that story," explained Asher.

"Well, that's how he died… Chasin' the gold."

"Nobody's ever went lookin' for gold since?" Asher questioned with disbelief.

"Nope. Legend has it the mountain's cursed."

"Cursed?" Asher asked with contempt.

"Yup. Cursed," Claudie answered.

Claudie launched into the story. "After Ansylum died I took on some work repairin' a barn roof for an old Indian farmer that lived just a few miles out of town. The second day working on the roof it started to rain. The rain made the roof too slippery to work on. When I climbed down off the roof, the old Indian invited me up onto his porch for some coffee. We got to shootin' the breeze about where I last worked and the old Indian told me he knew just where I was talkin' about. Now mind you, I never said nothin' about the gold or the accident. I just told him about loggin' up there."

Claudie was getting more animated now as he began to tell the Indian's story.

"Well, then the old Indian launched into a story that his grandfather had told him. There was a favorite fishing hole up on the mountain that the local Indian people liked to fish. One day a young Indian brave was up there fishin' when an older boy from town of about eighteen, showed up to fish at the same spot. The boy from town was not Indian. The boy told the Indian he had no right to be fishin' there. Well, they went from exchangin' words to exchangin' blows and the boy from town lost his balance and fell into the creek. His head hit a rock when he landed. He never got up."

"Well, you can just imagine how the boy's family reacted to that, even though it was an accident. His relatives rounded up a posse to bring this Indian to justice.

The Indian boy was hiding out in the cave at the head of old Indian Creek with his three brothers. The posse found them up there in the cave and had them cornered."

"Both sides had guns. After hours of waiting, the Indian brothers decided to make a break for it. They came out guns blazin', but the posse had the drop on them. Before it was all done, all four of those Indian brothers were killed on that mountain."

"The Indian brothers that died that day had a grandfather that was a Mohawk medicine man. So, the medicine man put a curse on the mountain… *Anybody that tried to profit from that mountain would die a horrible death,"* Claudie said in a low dramatic tone.

"A curse? A horrible death? That's a pretty tall tale Claudie," Asher said exasperated with Claudie's obviously made up story.

"Maybe, but there's not a lot of earthquakes up in these parts," Claudie shot back with a kind of menacing grin.

Chapter 7

Adeline

Asher was mulling over what Claudie had said when his thoughts were suddenly halted with a clang. The cow bell attached to the inner front door bonged and the door swung open and SHE stepped in. Adeline Malinowski walked into his store.

"Holy...! What is she doing here?" Asher exclaimed in his head.

Adeline Malinowski was a girl in Asher's class. But not just any girl. She was the girl Asher has had a crush on since the fourth grade when she moved here from California. Asher had yet to even hardly speak to her in the last five years. She was way out of his league. She was beautiful and her father was a doctor and Asher was, well, poor. He felt his face go hot and his underarms begin to sweat.

Adeline walked up to the counter opposite to where Asher was standing. Asher could feel his heart beating hard in his chest.

"Hey Asher," Adeline chimed in her sweet musical voice.

"Hey Adeline," Asher croaked with nervousness.

Everyone called her Addie even though Asher really loved the name Adeline. Adeline was about as tall as Asher with a slight but muscular build. She ran track and cross-country. Asher had seen her running through town a few times this summer, blonde ponytail swinging side to side in perfect cadence. Asher was completely enamored with her.

"How's your summer going?" Adeline asked with possibly a hint of enthusiasm.

"Oh. Um, good. Uh, I got a new bike," Asher said awkwardly wishing he could take back his words a soon as they left his mouth.

"That was so stupid," Asher thought to himself.

"Oh, that's nice," Adeline offered, not really knowing how to respond.

"My mom needs some canning lids. She's making jam," Adeline informed him.

"Ya. Um, they're upstairs with the cannin' stuff," Asher explained.

"Of course there with the canning stuff. Duh! Why am I so dumb?" Asher thought to himself with disgust.

"I'll show you. Follow me," Asher instructed nervously.

Claudie was still standing at the counter not too far from Adeline. He looked at her then at Asher. He noted Asher's infatuated gaze, and gave him a knowing grin and nod.

"I guess I'll be going. I'll see you folks later," Claudie announced with a wink.

Claudie nodded at Adeline and toddled out the front door to rummage in his wagon once more.

Asher made his way to the ancient staircase that led to the second floor of the general store with Adeline in tow. She followed him up the creaking stairs to the canning isle.

"Do you need wide mouth or regular size lids?" Asher asked.

"I don't know. I'll just take a box of each," Adeline decided.

"Okay. You can return whatever you don't need," Asher offered.

"Okay. That works," Adeline said with satisfaction.

They turned and headed back to the staircase. Adeline lead this time. Asher followed her down the stairs noticing the muscle definition in her thigh as she descended. Her wonderful fragrance drifted behind her causing Asher to breathe deeply, drinking in her scent. Her blonde hair swayed half way down her back. He was completely enamored.

Asher entered the price of the canning lids into the ancient cash register with cha-chings and told Adeline the total it displayed. Adeline reached into her cut-off jean's pocket and pulled out a five. She tossed it on the counter. Asher snatched it up then retrieved her change from the cash drawer.

As he handed Adeline her change, his fingertips brushed her palm. Asher felt a flash of electric shock between them. But it was not a static shock. It was more like an intense tingle that traveled up his arm and settled in his chest. It was not painful but somehow desirable. Asher breathed in quick and deep, involuntarily.

Adeline smiled but did not betray if she had felt what Asher had felt. Asher was lost in Adeline's pale blue eyes for a moment, then snapped out of it.

"There you go. Bring back the size lids you don't need," Asher said trying to hide his infatuation.

"Okay. Thanks Asher. I'll see you later," Adeline said as she walked towards the door.

"Yup, see you later," Asher answered hoping it would be sooner rather then later. Asher watched her walk out the door than moved to the front window to watch her walk down the street and out of sight. Totally enamored.

Asher looked down at his discount sneakers. He remembered someone saying on one of those detective shows that he loved to watch, that you could tell a lot from a person's shoes.

Working at E. M. Marley & Co. this summer, Asher has sold shoes and boots to all different kinds of people and he had found that a person's shoe does indeed reveal much about themselves.

An affluent person wore an expensive brand name shoe. If the name brand shoes are tattered, that person is thrifty, trying to get every bit of good out of them. If someone is wearing the newest style, they are worried about what people think of them. If they are wearing discount clothes but expensive shoes, they are likely living above their means trying to impress. It's easier to pass off clothing as high end but impossible to fake an expensive name brand sneaker.

And of course shoes can give away your occupation and hobbies. A carpenter that builds houses wears a certain kind of work shoe that has to be comfortable because he is on his feet all day. Preferably a soft sole that will grip slippery roofing steel and damp framing lumber alike.

A logger actually has a style of boot named for him. A "logger" work boot has deep tread with a two-inch chunk heel and is usually waterproof. The heel allows him to stand on a log as he limbs it.

A milk farmer lives in rubber boots because she is always in wet and slop and the cow manure eats up any other material. And there were a thousand other inferences that could be deduced from people and their footwear.

These are all generalizations of course and there are always exceptions. Asher knew of one type of footwear that had no exceptions. If someone was wearing discount sneakers, it was because they could not afford something better. Nobody would wear them on purpose. Asher scowled at his cheap footwear.

"Adeline has the latest Nike running shoe. That pretty much sums it up, doesn't it?" He fumed to himself.

Asher had always been taught that money can't buy happiness. And he supposed that was true in some cases, but not an absolute. He thought quite a bit about this topic. He figured that he thought about it much more than the average fourteen-year-old.

If you are terminally ill or horribly injured, no amount of money is going to help you. But, on the other hand, if you are miserable because your starving to death, well some wealth will go a long way toward your happiness.

Asher also had been drilled to strive for a better life, which implied trying to make a lot of money. The contradiction was obvious to Asher at an early age. He finally decided on a compromising mantra. *"Money might not necessarily bring you happiness, but it helps."* With the Adeline situation, Asher thought wealth was absolutely going to help.

"Just what is gold worth?" Asher asked himself.

He remembered seeing something in the Wall Street Journal about gold prices. He was not in the habit of reading that paper but Old Man Marley left it on the desk in back all of the time. When Asher was alone in the store with no customers, he sometimes would sit in the high stool and read the Journal. Probably not unlike generations of Marleys that had sat in that same stool before him.

Asher sat in the high stool and pulled the Journal in front of him. He looked at the date at the top of the paper; August 23, 1980. It was a couple of days old but Asher did not think that would matter. He skimmed through the pages of the paper until he found what he was looking for; $594.90 per ounce. Asher sat there staring at the numbers allowing this information to sink in.

Four sticks of butter make up a pound. There are sixteen ounces in a pound. Gold is much denser than butter so a brick of gold would be much smaller than a box of butter. Maybe half as big. Sixteen times almost $600 is $9600.

"That can't be right," he whispered aloud with disbelief.

He reached for the Texas Instruments calculator that sat on the desk and punched in the numbers 594.9 times 16 equals 9,518.4. Asher stared at the green lighted numbers on the calculator with his jaw dropped.

Asher hopped off the stool and made for the converted oak icebox where the milk and butter was kept.

He lifted its corroded handle to unlatch the door and swung it open. He retrieved a pound box of butter and held it in both hands. Almost 10,000 dollars if this box of butter were gold. He let that sink in, and then the excitement in his chest rose to almost uncontained.

Chapter 8

Old Man Marley

Old Man Marley shuffled through the store's back door.

"Somebody need some butter?" He gruffed at Asher with eyebrows furrowed to a deep crease.

"Um. No. I was just checkin' the uh expiration date," Asher explained trying to act casual.

"Any customers?" Old Man Marley barked impatiently.

"Um. Ya, one. She got cannin' lids," Asher offered.

"Did you sell her a case of jars and a new graniteware canner?" Old Man Marley interrogated.

Old Man Marley was not kidding. If he would have waited on Adeline, he would have attempted to sell her all of that and socks too. No matter how much money Adeline's mother sent her with, he would have gotten her to spend it all. Asher speculated that Old Man Marley is where the phrase "he could sell ice to an Eskimo" came from.

"Um. No, but I tried to," Asher lied, hoping Old Man Marley would drop the subject.

Old Man Marley was a grump and solely focused on making a sale. Asher didn't really like him at first, but not long after he started working there he realized Old Man Marley was a fair and kind boss but with a hard exterior. Once Asher got by Old Man Marley's quirky and gruff personality, Asher realized that he meant well.

"Have you swept the floor yet?" Marley asked dropping the inquisition of the morning's sale.

"No, but I was just about to," Asher explained.

With that, Old Man Marley turned his attention to the new Wall Street Journal that he had tucked under his arm. He had been ranting one minute and then engrossed in the financial news of the day in the next. He was not eloquent with transitions and did not bother much with pleasantries. Asher had finally grown accustom to his jerky jumping from one topic to another.

Asher swept, and mopped, and dusted, and stocked shelves, and ran to the post office, and everything else Old Man Marley wanted him to do. He was busy all day and it made the time fly by.

At ten minutes before five o'clock Asher retrieved his camping supplies from under the counter and carefully packed them in his backpack. Old Man Marley was next door at his house eating supper, leaving Asher alone again in the store. Asher went over the supply list in his head, making sure he was not forgetting anything.

"Maybe a lighter? That would be better than matches," He thought to himself.

Asher chose a blue Bick lighter and rang it through the register. Any chain store would never let an employee cash himself out, but E. B. Marley & Co. was no chain and this was definitely a perk of Asher's job.

Marley returned at 5:15 mumbling about high oil prices. Asher politely listened to him vent as he walked towards the back door to leave.

"Okay. I'll see you next week Mr. Marley." Asher said trying to end Old Man Marley's rant so he could leave for home.

"Ya. See you next week," Marley finally concluded and Asher was out the back door.

Asher slung his black nylon backpack onto his back, adjusting the contents for minimum annoyance for the bike ride home. He kicked the Spalding road bike's kickstand up and mounted the bike. He pedaled down the old driveway, swerving around potholes and then turned out onto Main Street. He bent over the handle bars and pushed hard on the pedals, speeding towards home.

Approaching the last house on the edge of town Asher caught a glimpse of Adeline climbing the stairs to her house. He braked without thinking as he watched the white aluminum screen door close behind her with a swish and bang. She was, well, wow.

He suddenly realized he had almost rolled to a stop. Snapping out of his trance, he resumed his muscle burning pace out of town toward supper. He bumped and rattled his way along the six miles of country road. As he pedaled along, he rehearsed the coming exchange with his mother.

Chapter 9

The Garden

Asher rolled into his driveway, confident that he would be able to convince his mother to let him stay with Uncle Jeb. He opened the back door and awkwardly carried his bike down the steps to the basement where he stored it, keeping it safe from the elements. Asher trotted up the stairs taking two at a time.

"Hi Mom. Is supper ready?" Asher asked.

"Almost. You can set the table," his mother answered matter-of-factly.

"Okay. Did I tell you Uncle Jeb wants me to stay with him a couple of nights so I can help him work on his porch? That porch is ready to fall off the front of the cabin," Asher said with as much everyday nonchalance as he could muster.

Asher's mother looked up from the hamburgers cooking in an old non-stick frying pan that long since had become an all-stick frying pan.

"When does he want you to stay over?" She asked with a little shock as this was the first she had heard of Uncle Jeb's request.

"Well I could go tomorrow and stay into the weekend. I don't have to work at Marley's for the rest of the week," Asher replied just as he had rehearsed in his head.

"What about the garden? The beans need pickin' tomorrow and the whole garden needs weedin'," Asher's mother informed him.

Asher expected this protest and had an answer ready, "I'll get up early and get all that done before I leave."

"What about the lawn mowing?" Asher's mother retorted.

"I can do it when I get back on Sunday," Asher said with rehearsed confidence.

Asher's mother, exhausted with the exchange, finally gave in, "I guess you can go tomorrow after your chores are done but make sure you're home by Sunday morning."

"Thanks Mom. I'll be home early Sunday morning." Asher said trying to exude gratitude without giving away his excitement.

Asher's mother returned her attention to the more than done hamburgers cooking on the stovetop. She snatched the pan off the burner and placed it on a hot mat that she kept by the stove to protect the Formica countertop.

"Time to eat," She proclaimed.

Asher happily finished setting the table while turning over the next day's events in his head. Tomorrow his adventure begins.

Asher was, as a rule, not an early riser. But today was the day his adventure would begin. The earlier he got started on his chores, the earlier he could leave for Uncle Jeb's cabin.

He had picked bushels and bushels of beans, starting as early as four years old, helping his father with the harvest. Asher was fast and thorough at the task, and he soon had a white five-gallon bucket almost filled to the top.

"Okay. On to the weeds," he sighed to himself.

He crouched down between the rows, using both hands to yank the weeds and clumps of grass from the earth. Asher was unfortunately an expert at this chore, logging in hundreds of hours through the years. His parent's garden took up half of the almost acre lot they lived on. That is a lot of rows of vegetables.

Asher stood up and stepped out of the corn patch to survey the rest of the garden, trying to determine how much work was left to do. He had five more rows of potatoes and then he would be finished. The morning air was still and thick. As he stepped out of the rows of corn into the rows of potatoes, Asher was exposed to the full intensity of the August sun. He was being baked, and the heat slowed him down considerably.

The sweat ran down his forehead stinging his eyes. His t-shirt was drenched. His mind wandered to years earlier and afternoons spent with his father in the garden. At the time, Asher resented being made to work in the garden instead of being allowed to play in the woods out back. Asher had an ongoing camp building project at that time, and he had thought it had needed his constant attention. The garden was always cutting into his camp play time.

Asher and his father spent those afternoons bent, and crouched, and sweating, and yanking, and picking, and hilling, and watering, but not much was said by either one. Asher eventually came to realize the value in the effort. But it was not just the effort that produced the satisfaction of the harvest.

Asher realized the underlying theme was grit. Actually not the underlying theme, but at the forefront. The most important lesson that he had learned in those hours of sweat and exhaustion, was the value of grit. Not everything is fun in life, and sometimes buckling down and doing the hard thing is worth it later. Asher has found this lesson serves him well in life.

The unending rows of weeds finally ended. Asher pulled the last weed from the last row with satisfaction and anticipation. He had finished his mundane chores and it was time to get started on his quest.

Chapter 10

The Journey Begins

Asher descended the basement stairs to his bedroom where his backpack was lying in wait, full of the camping supplies that he had packed the night before. Everything fit in the backpack except his sleeping bag, the pick, and the shovel.

He lashed the sleeping bag to the backpack with some old cotton clothesline he had found hanging next to his father's workbench. Next he slid the rusty pick axe he had gotten out of the garden shed between the sleeping bag and backpack, positioning the metal end up.

"That should stay," he thought to himself.

Then he did the same with the short handled, round pointed shovel, that he had also retrieved from the garden shed.

Asher slung the backpack conglomeration over his shoulder and onto his back. It felt heavy and awkward as he bent forward to steady himself.

"This is going to be a long trek up to the cave," Asher said with realization.

He climbed the gloomy basement stairs to the blinding daylight of the mid-morning sun.

As he stood in the doorway, Asher called to his mother toiling in the kitchen canning beans. "I'm all done weeding. I'm headed to Uncle Jeb's now."

Asher's mother answered with exhausted concern, "Be careful. I'll see you Sunday morning. Call me if you need anything."

"Okay. I will," Asher promised.

He awkwardly closed the back door behind him trying to balance the heavy pack on his back.

"This is not gonna work," Asher decided out loud.

He slung the pack off his back down to the ground. He studied it. He finally decided that he needed to move the shovel and pickaxe as far to either side of the pack as he could. Hopefully this would better distribute the weight. After making the changes to his pack, he slung it over his shoulders again.

"That's better," Asher proclaimed to himself then started for the barbwire fence.

He attempted to hold the top strand down and climb over but he just was not tall enough for the maneuver. Off his pack came again with a sigh and he placed it on the ground on the other side of the fence. Then he pushed the middle wire down so he could climb through.

As he bent to cross the fence he suddenly remembered he needed his fishing pole. The plan was to tell Uncle Jeb that he was going camping upstream to fish. Uncle Jeb was old but he was still pretty sharp. He would notice that Asher did not have a fishing pole for his venture.

Asher jogged back to the house to retrieve his fishing pole. As he made his exit carrying his fishing pole his mother met him at the door.

"What do you need that for? I thought you were helping to fix the porch," his mother inquired impatiently.

"I am. I just thought I might have a few minutes to cast in right by the cabin in the evenings," Asher falsely explained as he tried to sound reasonable.

"Well don't be goofin' off. You're there to help your Uncle Jeb. Not to fish," his Mother scolded.

"I know. I won't get my pole out unless we're done for the day," Asher promised

"Okay. Be careful and do what Uncle Jeb says," Asher's mother instructed.

"I will," Asher promised. "I'll see you Sunday."

"See you Sunday," Asher's mother said with an exhausted tone.

With that Asher made for the fence once again. He dipped between the strands of barbwire and snatched up his pack. The fishing pole did not separate into two pieces so it was too long to attach to his backpack. Asher opted to just hold it in his left hand for now. He could ditch it as soon as he was out of sight of Uncle Jeb's cabin.

He was exploding with anticipation and his quick pace, despite the heavy pack, reflected his mood.

"This is gonna be so great," he said aloud with excitement, "even if I only find ten ounces that's still almost six thousand dollars worth of gold."

Asher made his way upstream towards Uncle Jeb's cabin at almost a jog. It was relatively easy going and the thoughts of gold riches propelled him even quicker.

As he drew nearer to Uncle Jeb's place, he began to rehearse the upcoming conversation with Uncle Jeb in his head. The only problem was that Uncle Jeb was much less predictable then his mother. Asher tried his best to anticipate different responses from his uncle, but he knew in the end that he would likely have to improvise.

He rounded the final bend before Uncle Jeb's cabin. As he approached, his chest suddenly tightened as he realized he had overlooked a potentially big problem. He was not going to be able to explain away the shovel and pickaxe to Uncle Jeb and they would not go unnoticed. Asher stopped in his tracks.

Uncle Jeb's rocking chair sat on an angle, faced slightly away from Asher's approach.

"Did he see me?" Asher murmured to himself.

He stood stock still for a long moment studying Uncle Jeb's profile. It was unchanging. The cadence of Uncle Jeb's rocking chair was as unchanging as a metronome.

Asher sighed with relief as he slowly crouched down into the weeds and brush. He dropped his backpack and pole to the ground, then slowly slid the pickaxe and shovel out from between his sleeping bag and backpack.

Asher knew that the movement might prompt Uncle Jeb to look his way. Unexpected movements could even prompt Uncle Jeb to start blasting with his shotgun. That was a scenario Asher needed to avoid.

Asher stayed crouched, using the underbrush as cover. Slowly, with the shovel and pickaxe in each hand, he back tracked a hundred yards beyond the bend in the creek. He pulled out his compass. The creek ran generally north, so Asher needed to head directly north east to approach the cabin on the back side and make his way around it without being seen.

It was hard going as he bush-whacked straight through the woods, but he finally made it to the seasonal maintenance road that ran to the front of the cabin, opposite the porch. Asher took another reading from his compass and then set out on a north west heading hoping to run into the creek sooner rather than later. After fifteen minutes he spotted a clearing through the dense brush.

"The creek." Asher said aloud with accomplishment.

And sure enough the creek lay directly ahead. He figured he was only a couple of hundred yards from the cabin, but there was another sharp bend in the creek, so he could not see it from where he stood.

"Perfect," he said to himself with satisfaction. "Now where to hide these until I come back up through?"

Asher looked the area over and decided on a huge boulder protruding out into the creek. It looked almost out of place there, so he knew he would be able to find it again. He used the shovel to clear away the dead leaves and pine needles down to the dirt at the base of the boulder. He placed the pickaxe and shovel in the dirt and then covered them over with the leaves and pine needles. He picked up two small branches from the ground and laid them in an "x" over the spot.

"That should do it," Asher proclaimed with confidence. "Now back around to the other side of the cabin."

It had occurred to Asher that he could have just hiked around the cabin and leave Uncle Jeb out of the plan all together, but it seemed too risky. If his mother did call to check on him, Uncle Jeb could tell her that he had been there, but he was up fishing. That might cause her to be disgusted with him, but at least it would not prompt a call to the police or a launch of a search party. Besides, Asher also thought it might not be a bad idea if someone actually knew where he would be, in case he ran into some kind of trouble.

Asher made his way back around to the other side of the cabin, with considerable less difficulty, and came to rest where his pack and fishing pole lay in the brush. He retrieved his backpack and slung it once more on his back. With his fishing pole in hand, Asher trudged up to Uncle Jeb's cabin.

Chapter 11

Rabbit Stew

Creak… creak… creak… "Hey Uncle Jeb," Asher greeted him loudly as he approached.

"Hey Asher. How goes it today?" Uncle Jeb croaked like someone that had not spoken in days because he had not.

The smoke from his pipe drifted lazily up into the porch rafters and beyond, into the surrounding treetops.

"Good. Really good," Asher announced with almost too much enthusiasm.

"What were you doin' wandering around in the woods out in front of the cabin?" Uncle Jeb asked drawing a knowing, nearly toothless grin across his face.

Creak…creak… creak…

"How could he have known that? He didn't see me. He was just sittin' there rockin' and not movin'. He hadn't moved from that chair. Had he?" The questions swirled silently through Asher's mind.

"Um. Well, I saw some, uh turkeys and I was followin' them… until they took off," Asher stammered.

"You're not gonna catch a turkey by hand. You need one of these," he said matter-of-factly as he grabbed his shotgun and aimed it at nothing Asher could see.

Uncle Jeb had to be almost a hundred years old but he moved with lightning speed as he went for his shotgun and drew a bead on no particular target across the creek.

Bang! Bang! Both barrels of Uncle Jeb's shotgun suddenly unloaded on a bush across the creek. Asher's heart nearly stopped as he gasped aloud. The gun's explosion left Asher's ears ringing with a momentary deafness. The smoke from the old gun filled the air on the porch, and the smell of gunpowder and pipe tobacco hung heavy.

"Did I scare ya?" Uncle Jeb asked with not too much concern in his voice. "Dinner's over there in the brush."

"I didn't see anything," Asher protested as he shook his head trying to clear the ringing in his ears.

"Sure. Do-it-yourself rabbit stew. Go over there and fetch it and see for yourself," Uncle Jeb directed.

Asher took off across the creek dropping his pack with his first step. He was still breathing hard from the shock of the blast. He skipped over the rocks and was to the other side in a moment.

The fine branches and leaves of the alder bush were blown away where the buckshot spread had hit. Asher bent down and peered into the gap in the brush. Sure enough, there was a dead cottontail laid sprawled in the dirt. There was a hole in the rabbit's neck where a pellet from the buckshot pierced the fur.

Asher had no idea how Uncle Jeb had seen that rabbit let alone hit him, even if it did take two shots. He reached through the shattered branches and grasped a back leg of the dead rabbit. He pulled the limp carcass out and stood up, revealing it to Uncle Jeb.

Asher's father was not a hunter, so in turn Asher was not either. Hunting seemed to be a generational and traditional pastime. Somehow the tradition ended with Asher's father. But Asher did know quite a bit about hunting for the simple fact that almost everyone Asher knew was a hunter of some sort. If a person lived in this county, they were immersed in the hunting culture, whether they participated or not.

Asher did not have a problem with hunting. How could he? After all he ate meat without discrimination. He had an appreciation for the skill it took for Uncle Jeb to be able make that shot, but personally, he just did not like killing things. Perhaps a trait he inherited from his father.

The closest Asher had come to the sport was pinging old soda cans off fence posts with his Daisy pump-for-power bb/pellet air rifle. Asher actually loved to target practice on cans or the occasional glass bottle if he could find one along the road to shatter. He was a pretty good shot, considering the limitations of a bb gun. Maybe that was a trait he inherited from Uncle Jeb.

"Yup. Rabbit stew for dinner," Uncle Jeb said with satisfaction.

Asher returned across the creek with the game and carried it up onto the porch to present to Uncle Jeb. He laid it out on the rickety old picnic table that sat sagging at the far end of the porch.

Uncle Jeb took a good long look at the rabbit and then displayed a contented smirk with a little twinkle in his eye. After all these years he could still hit his mark and provide sustenance for himself.

"Are you gonna' stay for dinner? They'll be plenty of stew for both of us," Uncle Jeb offered hopefully.

Asher reluctantly broke the news to Uncle Jeb. "Well, uh, I'm headed upstream campin'. To fish the east branch."

"Is that so? All by yourself?" Uncle Jeb said skeptically.

"Ya. I didn't really have time to fish up there last time because it took so long to hike up the creek," Asher explained as he realized this conversation was not really going as rehearsed.

"The east branch, right?" Uncle Jeb asked with a warning tone.

"Ya. The east branch. What's the problem with the west branch anyways?" Asher hesitantly asked hoping to get some sort of confirmation of Claudie's story.

"There's no fish in the west branch and its bad luck up there anyways," Uncle Jeb answered with a vagueness that did not satisfy Asher's curiosity.

"Why is it bad luck?" Asher asked, wondering if he already knew the answer.

"There's been accidents up there. Accidents that can only be explained by bad luck. Everybody steers clear of the west branch." Uncle Jeb chided with enough resolve that Asher knew not to pursue the line of questioning.

"I'm plannin' to set up my tent just beyond the fork in the creek on the east branch. There's a clearing up there," Asher explained hoping to diffuse the tension.

"Yup. That would be a good spot," Uncle Jeb agreed. How long are you gonna' stay up there?"

"Til' Sunday morning probably," Asher said confidently.

"That's a long time by yourself. Are you gonna' be okay up there all alone?" Uncle Jeb said with genuine concern. "Do you want me to come up and check on you Saturday morning?"

"Nah. I'll be fine," Asher assured him knowing it was an empty offer. Uncle Jeb had not been farther than a couple hundred yards from his cabin in years as far as Asher knew.

"Well, okay. I'll be lookin' for you Sunday morning. If you run into trouble, you come back here straight away," Jeb advised expressing uncharacteristic concern.

"Alright. Um, I will," not knowing quite what to make of Uncle Jeb's new-found protectiveness. "I probably should get going so I have plenty of time to set up camp before dark."

"Yup. Probably you should. I got to get to skinnin' this rabbit." Uncle Jeb said with a grin.

"Okay. Well I'll see you Sunday morning then," Asher said as he slung his backpack on his back with an audible humph and picked up his fishing pole.

"See ya Sunday," Uncle Jeb said as he was contemplating the rabbit laid out on the cedar planks of the old picnic table.

He clearly had shifted focus from Asher's lone trek to the skinning and dressing of his dinner. Uncle Jeb had his pocket knife in hand and was shuffling over towards the rabbit as Asher strode away from the cabin upstream. In minutes Asher was around the bend of the creek beyond Uncle Jeb's line of sight.

He quickly spotted the boulder that he had buried the shovel and pickaxe beside. He swiped the leaves and pine needles off the tools and then stuffed them in between the backpack and sleeping bag. He hoisted the awkward pack into position on his back, teetering a little before finding his balance. He was off.

Chapter 12

Jumbo

Asher felt upbeat realizing he had plenty of time to reach his destination at the head of the west branch. He would be able to take his time and pick the easiest route. Or so he thought.

Asher marched along the creek feeling pretty good about executing his plan thus far. It did not go exactly as he had envisioned it, but he was still pretty much on schedule. He climbed a bank up away from the stream and began to descend.

As he took the second stride down the embankment he glanced up from his feet. A blur of orange squares lined the gully and Asher dropped to the ground flat. The contents of his backpack slammed into his back as he hit the forest floor. Simultaneously a thick pine root smashed into his sternum. Despite the pain he did not dare cry out.

Asher had been so caught up in the joy of the moment that he almost walked obliviously into Barker territory. He lay still, partially shrouded by some large ferns, listening. A downy wood pecker chattered in a nearby decaying tree, but nothing else.

Asher inched his way backward to the crest of the knoll on his belly until he reached the summit and then dropped down on the other side, out of site from the Barker posters. He laid there contemplating his next move. The whole "running after he thought the coast was clear thing" did not really work all that well last time. He needed another strategy.

He shed his pack and rolled to his back facing the deep blue bowl of the summer sky. Just then a red tailed hawk floated overhead, screaming his rapture call. The bird of prey caught an up-draft and soared upward like a fighter jet.

"If I were up there I could see if the Barker brothers were in the area," Asher thought to himself.

That gave Asher an idea. He stood up slowly and surveyed the trees at the top of the ridge. A big old white pine that was all branches stood on its own, towering above the surrounding trees. It was perfect for climbing and would provide great cover. He inched towards the trunk of the massive tree, staying low and hopefully out of site.

Asher reached up and grasped the first branch he could reach. He pulled himself up in a chin-up motion and at the same time he used the trunk of the tree to walk the lower half of his body upward. In a moment he was standing on the first lower branch. From there it was just a matter of climbing the tree like you would a jungle gym. The branches were close enough to serve as irregular rungs, and Asher made his way to the top in no time.

He climbed up and up until he encountered branches that were of questionable strength to hold his body weight. Asher had been climbing pine trees his whole life and he was completely comfortable swaying up there in the pine boughs.

From his lofty vantage point the view was amazing. Asher could see for miles in all directions. But most importantly, he could see the Barker's claimed land and the brothers seemed to be nowhere in sight. He breathed in deep to take in the fresh pine pitch smell then carefully began to descend.

When he had climbed about half way down the immense old tree, some movement in the pines directly ahead of him caught Asher's eye. He instinctively froze in place, both of his hands grasping a limb over his head and one foot on the next limb below. His other foot was in midair, stopping its search for the next limb. Motionless and breathless he scanned the area where he had thought he saw a movement.

It is an evolutionary reflex for prey to freeze when encountering a perceived danger, as movement stimulates detection, and chase in a predator. Asher's prey instinct had kicked in.

He strained his eyes and ears with intensity. A snap of a branch, a rustle of brush, a glimpse of black, a faint low grunt, fur... a black bear. It lumbered out of the ferns and saplings into a slight clearing revealing its entire hulking body. Asher was hit like a truck with a wave of adrenaline. He had never encountered a black bear out in the woods alone.

Asher knew that there were black bears in the area. One had tried to break into Uncle Jeb's cabin earlier that month. The Bear did not get in, as the cabin had long since been bear-proofed. But the scratch marks on the solid plank cabin door from the bear's huge claws and the black hairs scattered around the porch revealed its attempt. There has been black bear living in these woods long before any human settlement.

The bear sniffed unceasingly like a bloodhound hot on the trail of escaped convicts. It paused and raised its massive head pointing its probing snout skyward. With a slight rock back, it stood up humanlike and effortlessly, holding its front furry paws in front itself like a dog begging for a treat. But this was no dog. It stood almost seven feet tall, all claws and matted brownish black fur. Its bulky muscles rippled beneath the layer of fat that the bear had been tirelessly adding to for the winter hibernation.

Asher stayed motionless as he tracked the movements of the bear. He watched it sniff the air and Asher was suddenly concerned with the direction of the breeze. The warm early afternoon air hit Asher in the face confirming he was upwind of the immense black bear that had ambled into his path.

"He probably can't smell me," Asher nervously reasoned to himself.

The bear dropped back down to all four paws and resumed his stroll through the woods sampling all of the scents in the air as he went. Asher slowly moved his dangling leg back up to the tree branch where his other foot rested and stood perfectly still trying to become part of the old pine tree.

Asher watched with dread as the bear moved ever closer toward him. He could hear him grunting, and sniffing, and cracking twigs, closer, and closer. The bear wandered to only a few feet from the base of the tree that cloaked Asher as he clung to the opposite side. The bear stopped just short of the base of the pine tree sampling the air as Asher clung frozen with fear.

Asher heard the awful scratching of claws on the opposite side of the tree. Black bears are excellent tree climbers and Asher held his breath waiting for the bear to be upon him. He could actually smell the musky wild scent of the bear.

Suddenly the bear dropped back to all four paws again. And just like that, it meandered off to the west and disappeared into the underbrush, leaving Asher quivering with fear as he clung to the towering tree. Asher exhaled with a huge sigh of relief as soon as the bear was out of sight. A black bear's eye sight is not that great and the bear apparently had not caught Asher's scent either.

Asher closed his eyes and tried to will his heart rate to decelerate. He took deep breaths and exhaled slowly.

"That was just too close," Asher whispered to himself.

He scrambled down the balance of the tree with adrenaline still pumping through his veins. Asher crouched at the base, leaning on the trunk, contemplating his next move.

Asher reasoned the black bear was headed to an immense blackberry patch that was located not far from

Uncle Jeb's cabin. He had spent many hours picking berries in that patch summer afternoons years before. The briars would be loaded with dark, fat, ripe berries this time of year. With the bear likely working on its winter stores and the Barker brothers apparently not in the area, Asher cautiously decided to traverse the disputed gully.

Slowly and carefully he made his way to his pack in a crouch. He grasped the nylon strap of his pack and shimmied it over his shoulders and on to his back. Asher slunk back to the crest of the knoll and paused one more time to listen and scan the woods.

"It's bad enough I have to keep an eye out for the Barker Brothers. Now I have Jumbo Bear to worry about?" Asher asked himself wearily.

Asher crept down the embankment passing the first line of posted signs guarding the imaginary border. "So far, so good." He passed the second line of Barker posters without incident and then he was on Mason land again.

Chapter 13

The Old Homestead

The fact that his family owned hundreds of acres of land made Asher smile with pride. The Mason land was originally split evenly between Uncle Jeb and his siblings, but now he was the last remaining member of that family still living. Uncle Jeb had inherited all of it.

Asher thought he had remembered his father saying Uncle Jeb now would own over seven hundred acres of land now that Great Grandpa Mason passed away. Asher's father also had mentioned at that time that he did not know how Uncle Jeb would pay taxes on all of that land. Somehow Uncle Jeb must be keeping up on the land tax though. He still owned the land and his name had not been in the paper for late taxes.

Asher was feeling better about his adventure now that he was past the Barker's posters and he relaxed a little as he trudged along the creek.

"Almost ten thousand dollars a pound." What would he do with all that money?

A more pressing question was; how would he cash it in? Technically the state would own whatever he found. Asher was convinced there had to be a way around New York State confiscating the family's gold. Asher reasoned that he would "cross that bridge when, and if, he came to it."

After walking for some distance with his awkward backpack, Asher was fast approaching the swamp. He had plenty of daylight left so he chose to avoid the swamp all together. Instead of descending into the beaver swale, Asher chose the high ground to the east.

"No sense in braving that muck hole when I've got plenty of time," Asher reasoned.

He hiked east skirting the swamp. He clambered ever higher to stay well out of the low land. Asher realized he was in an area that he had never been through before. The other times when he went around the swamp he had stayed to the west of it. His head was on a swivel taking in the new scenery. He tried to pick out landmarks as he went and file them away for future reference.

The dense underbrush and mature trees gave way to a narrow clearing. Saplings populated the space but no large trees. Asher stood in the clearing surveying his surroundings. The slim open space stretched behind him and onward.

"An old road," Asher speculated, "probably an old logging road."

The old road seemed to be traveling in generally the same direction as Asher needed to go, so he took advantage of the path. As he rambled along the remnants of the ancient road, he noticed rocks piled neatly along the edge.

"Why is there a rock wall way out here on a logging road?" Asher puzzled to himself.

Rock walls were found on land that the earlier generations had cleared for farming. These woods looked far too old for ever having been farm land. As he continued on the path, the rock walls were more and more prominent removing any doubt that the surrounding land had been farmed long ago.

Asher abruptly stopped in the middle of the old woods road to watch a rare black squirrel scamper down a tall pine tree stump. The top half of the rest of the pine tree lay on the ground nearby, apparently severed by a lightning strike earlier that summer.

The black squirrel was actually a dark smoky color and, as far as Asher knew, it was just a color variation of a grey squirrel, but it was quite rare to see one. He watched the nervous squirrel dart from tree, to tree, to rock, to tree, to fence post?...

"A fence post? Way out here in the middle of the woods?" Asher broke from the trail to investigate.

He approached the decayed cedar post as he watched the squirrel dart away, disappearing into the woods. As Asher scrutinized the fence post he could see bits of badly rusted barbwire still pinched under the fence staples. From the location of the remnants of the barbwire, Asher could deduce which direction the fence once ran.

He dropped his pack and held his arms straight out from his sides so his body created a "T". He oriented his arms to run parallel with where he imagined the fence used to be. He picked a land mark that aligned with his left arm then took a bearing with his compass of northeast. Asher reasoned that he could find more of the fading fence line by following that compass bearing. He slung his pack back over his shoulders.

He ventured about a hundred feet northeast, scanning the rugged terrain for any sign of the old barbwire fence. He stopped at the base of a hard maple tree and stared at it, trying to decipher what he was seeing. There was a piece of barbwire about five feet off the ground that looked like it was growing directly from the center of the tree like a rusty barbed branch.

The tree must have served as a fence post many, many years ago. The barbwire likely was stapled to the maple tree. Over the years, as it grew, it engulfed the wire. The barbwire now penetrated right through the center of the trunk, protruding out of either side.

Asher continued on his northeast bearing beyond the barbwire maple tree finding more and more partial cedar fence posts and fragments of wire.

There was now enough fence that he put away his compass and he picked through the woods by just following the fence line. He was generally traveling in the direction he needed to go, so he continued down the fence line out of curiosity. If there used to be a fence here, then likely there used to be a farm with a barn and a house somewhere in the area.

Even if there were buildings that belonged to the fence line, Asher knew that they would have been reduced to piles of rubble long ago. Still, it might be interesting to explore the remains. As he thought about what he might find, Asher abruptly came to a stop. He could no longer discern where the fence was. He surveyed the area.

Asher's eyes fixed on a depression in the ground to the east of the fence line that seemed to run in a straight line into a dense cluster of cedar trees. Straight lines were out of place in nature, and so he studied the landscape for a moment. Between the upper branches of the cedar trees, Asher thought he could make out what looked like moss. Possibly it was a massive boulder or a rock face that jutted up from the forest floor immediately beyond the cedar trees. The moss had to be growing on something high above the immediate ground-scape.

Asher dropped his pack to the ground in one motion and walked toward the cedars following the shallow depression in the terrain. As he drew nearer, he realized it was not a natural feature behind the trees... It was a building, or at least part of a building.

Asher parted the dense cedar branches and pushed his body through, back first. He spun one hundred and eighty degrees as he emerged on the other side of the cedar trees to face the towering building before him.

The enormous sagging structure shot skyward from the forest floor cutting a completely out of place profile in the thick wooded area. It was the remains of an ancient post and beam barn. The kind that were found all over the north eastern United States, dating as far back as colonial times. The barn's cedar shake roof was completely engulfed in fury moss that looked like the green shag carpet that Asher's parents had removed from their living room two years ago.

The roof of the crumpling building was actually only half there. The remainder of the cedar shakes and roof boards lay on the hay loft floor or had been blown away as they decayed to dust many years ago. The immense timber that formed the framework of the structure stood mostly intact. The timbers were actually whole trees carved out in various areas with notches and flat spots so they could be locked and fitted together. Asher could still see where the limbs of the timbers had been expertly hacked off with a limbing axe.

The walls of the barn were missing more barn boards than what was left nailed to the framework, creating more of a suggestion of a wall. The remaining wall boards had just a hint of lingering red hue. Some of the boards were two feet wide which was a testament to the size of the trees that were logged in those days.

Asher approached the old barn with some caution. He knew there was no danger of the barn's framework collapsing. He had helped Uncle Jeb tear a barn like this down last year on his property. They had taken each beam and post down individually. The beams stayed in place almost until the last one was yanked down. The way these barns were built, they just did not collapse.

Asher was worried about the rotten floor boards. He entered by first stepping up on the rock foundation of a lateral post. The gnarly post shot up through a hay chute in the hay loft floor to meet the rafter truss. It was still solid and sturdy. Asher grasped the post with both hands and jumped up to wrap his legs around it. He shimmied up the post with the dexterity of a native islander climbing a coconut tree.

There were no wall boards attached to this post and Asher clambered up all the way to the hay loft unimpeded. Once there, he swung a leg toward the questionable floor and applied some weight with his toes. It seemed solid so he swung his other leg to the hay loft floor and stood, still with a one hand grip on the post. This section of the floor was positioned under the part of the roof that was still intact. It must have shed enough water and weather through the years to keep the hay loft floor boards from deteriorating too bad.

Asher walked lightly from corner to corner of the remaining floor, testing the soundness with every step.

"I can't believe it's in this good of shape," Asher mused to himself.

As he gained confidence in the floor's structure, he began to move more freely and padded to the edge to peer down. Below there was a mangle of fragments of boards, and leaves, and pine needles, and cedar shakes, and pieces of branches, and rusty nails, and rusty spikes.

"Not a good place to land if I fall." Asher thought to himself. "I guess I better not fall."

It suddenly occurred to Asher that this might be an ideal place to set up camp rather than pitch his tent, especially with Jumbo prowling around. There was no way up to the loft except climbing the post that Asher had. That post would probably not work so well for that large of a bear. Besides, the floor would likely not hold old Jumbo's weight.

"Yup. I'm gonna sleep right up here," Asher announced out loud to himself.

He did not think he was too far from the split in the creek so it would be a short hike to the cave at the head of the west branch.

Asher began to inspect the loft for anything that might be of some use to him, or just of value in general. It was dim in the back corner of the barn and he waited a moment as his eyes adjusted. The silhouette of a rusty crosscut saw came into focus that was as long as Asher was tall. No doubt it had been worn past any usefulness long ago and then hung in loft because that generation never threw out anything.

Asher scanned the back wall until his eyes focused on a large roundish object hanging from a rafter. He drew nearer to determine if it was anything of value. He reached up and brushed the decades of dirt and cobwebs off it to reveal something that would be very useful to him.

It was a large wooden wheel pulley with a cast iron thimble and cheek. Although it was likely more than a hundred years old, Asher found that the wheel still turned freely. This would definitely be very useful, and in the near future.

He searched the space for anything else that he could use but there was nothing else to find except some badly frayed rope. The old barn had been stripped of anything of value long ago.

When Asher was satisfied there was nothing else to salvage he turned his attention to retrieving his backpack. He walked back to where the pulley hung and gripped it with both hands heaving it up off from the hand forged spike it hung on. It was not quite as heavy as he thought it would be as the wooden wheel was light and did not add much to its heft.

He carried it over to the edge of the hay loft where the floor ended. He had spotted another large spike that was drove into a rafter at about the right position to hang the pulley. He pressed the pulley up and over his head holding it in both hands. He stretched and waivered as he fished for the spike blindly. And then it slipped into place like it was made for that spot.

"Perfect," Asher said satisfied. "Now I'll go get my backpack."

He had rope in his pack that he could run up through the pulley and back down to the ground. He could use it to haul his pack up to the loft and anything else he needed. Asher made for the opening in the floor and struggled down the post to the rubble below.

"I need to figure out a better way up and down." Asher said to himself decidedly.

He jumped from the stone foundation and then trotted back toward his pack and fishing pole. As he moved quickly in the backpack's direction a sinking thought suddenly entered his head. His pack was full of food; namely peanut butter and jam sandwiches. There is nothing bears like better than peanut butter and jam sandwiches.

"How could I be that stupid?" Asher scolded himself aloud.

He quickened his pace but not to a run. He did not want to make an even bigger mistake by running up on a feeding bear. He now was completely focused on the huge potential problem that could, at the very least, end his adventure.

Chapter 14

The Well

Asher's heart pounded as he neared the spot where he had left his backpack. He stopped and surveyed the area in a crouch. No bear. He could have already been through and dragged the pack off. Asher could not see any sign of the pack from where he was, so he stalked slowly closer.

Snap! The sound of boards breaking shattered the silence of the forest as the ground disappeared out from under Asher's feet. Shards of rotten boards, and dirt, and leaves, and Asher, plunged into ice-cold water.

His feet smacked the water first and the rest of his body followed, plunging deep, to well over his head. More dirt and debris crashed down after him. The shock of the icy water made every muscle in his body contract as he held his breath through shear instinct. Down, down, down he plummeted for what felt like minutes but was really only a few seconds.

Without thinking, Asher kicked his legs hard and pulled his hands down from over his head. He repeated the motion, returning his arms over his head and back down in a breast stroke motion. Suddenly, his head bobbed above the water. He gasped, then choked and sputtered, trying to rid himself of the rancid water he had taken in.

Asher had fallen in the farm's hand dug well. Every homestead had one, and Asher had carelessly forgotten that fact. Over time, the leaves and vegetation build up around the hand laid stone foundation of the well, sometimes rendering it level with the ground. The sturdy wood planks that once formed the well's cover decay to a loosely adhered wood pulp as it too is buried by the seasons. Wells that were left unused and abandoned became invisible pit traps for unfortunate animals, or in some cases, people. Asher knew this. He had been warned many times about this danger.

Asher clung to the slimy granite stones that lined the pit as he tried to catch his breath and get his bearings. The air in the well hung heavy with decay and humidity. Though the water was likely about fifty degrees, it felt like ice-water to Asher when compared to the eighty-five degree August afternoon air. Asher almost immediately began to shiver and he knew he had to get out of that water soon, before hypothermia set in.

He peered up at the six foot opening far overhead. Asher estimated it must be at least twelve feet straight up. The light from the opening only provided a shaded view at the bottom of the well and he could just make out grey shadows of the stones that he grasped. It looked as though the stones maybe had enough space between them for finger and foot holds but this was going to be a treacherous free-climb.

Asher focused on the opening above, as his fingers and toes found a solid hold. He clamped on the slippery stones and propelled himself upward. He moved only a few inches toward the light but it was a start. He reached his right hand as high as he could, groping for a hand hold and found it. He pulled hard in a chin-up motion as he also used his legs to propel himself upward to ground level.

Hand hold then foothold. Again and again, he slowly and arduously made his way to the surface. Three feet from the top of the well, Asher grasped a brick size stone with his left hand and pulled against it to continue his ascent. The stone gave way and Asher nearly ended up at the bottom of the well again. He managed to stay himself at the last moment, clinging to the wall like Spiderman.

"That was close," Asher exclaimed to himself.

He continued his climb trying to brush off the latest close call. As he passed over the spot where the stone let loose, he noticed what looked like a void beyond the stone lining. He paused to investigate.

His right hand was clamped on a stone above and both feet were stuffed safely in crevasses between stones below. He reached his left hand into where the stone used to be and, sure enough, there was a hollow void beyond. As he searched the space, Asher hoped to himself that it was not a snake's den or worse that he was exploring.

He patted his hand around the void reaching ever farther into the earth. His hand finally touched on something. It was square, definitely manmade. He thrust his arm in farther until he was in almost to his shoulder and grasped the object. He slid it slowly out, still gripping the wall of the well.

It was a box about the size cigars come in but this box was crafted from wood, not cheap cardboard. It looked to be held closed with a thin leather strap tied around it. Asher stuffed the curious box under his arm and resumed climbing with this added difficulty. He inched his way up the last three feet and finally reached the surface.

Asher rolled up and onto the ground with more relief than he had ever felt before. He lay there panting with exhaustion and satisfaction from his ascent.

"The box!" Asher suddenly thought to himself with overwhelming excitement. "What's in the box?"

He rolled to his stomach holding the box in front of his face. He studied it for a moment. The thin leather strap definitely held the lid closed. Asher retrieved his Case pocket knife from his pocket and locked the blade open. He slid the blade under the leather strap and pulled up, slicing through it,

Asher lifted the now free lid. Inside there were ten shiny coins. They glinted in the sunlight as Asher held each one up. The coins were all identical, 1879 silver dollars.

"I wonder what these are worth now?" Asher asked himself. "They're probably made of real silver."

He turned the coins over in his fingers contemplating their worth. The only other thing in the box was a small brass skeleton key with a leather lanyard threaded through it. He picked up the key and inspected it closely. There were no markings on it.

As he placed the key back in the homemade wooden box, he noticed some faint writing on the inside of the lid of the box. Asher held it up to the sunlight straining his eyes to make out the scrawl.

If you read this
Than I am dead
And you have found my treasure

You're welcome to it
And the rest
If pickles are your pleasure

Take the key
Unlock the door
But it's not the one you guessed

Find the knot
The key fits in
And you'll find my treasure chest

Asher read it again, scrutinizing each word to assure himself that he was reading it correctly. Then he read it a third time aloud, hearing the rhythm in the prose. It was nonsensical.

"A riddle to a treasure? Really?" Asher asked himself. "Why couldn't it be a map? I'm terrible at riddles."

He read it over and over until he almost knew it by heart. It just made no sense to him. He could understand there was more treasure and he would need the key to find it, but that was about it. It suddenly dawned on Asher that the door the poem referred to was likely in the farm house that obviously was not standing any more. Asher had not yet even found the old house foundation where the house once stood. Even if he could solve the riddle the hidden treasure was likely buried under tons of rubble and years of decaying vegetation in the ruins of the long gone farm house.

Asher sighed with exasperation, "At least I won't come back empty handed," Asher thought to himself as fingered the silver dollars.

The sun was low in the pale pink sky now, just hovering above the tree line. Asher shivered as he realized he was still soaked to the skin and night was coming. His little adventure down the well had sealed his fate for the remainder of the day. He would travel no further and make camp right here at the old homestead.

Asher returned the silver coins to their little wooden box along with the key and tied it closed with what was left of the leather strap. He sprang to his feet, still grasping the box, as he remembered the backpack and peanut butter sandwiches and the possible looting bear. He needed to retrieve his pack and get a fire going so he could change his clothes and dry off.

With no sign of Jumbo, he took off toward where his pack and pole lay on the ground. As he approached the area, he spotted the pack then the pole, undisturbed, exactly where he had left it. He exhaled a sigh of relief knowing now his adventure would continue.

Asher retrieved the pack and pole and started back toward the old barn. He would build a fire pit using some stones from the crumbling foundation. His mind quickly returned to the rhyming riddle as he hiked back to his soon to be campsite.

He kept returning to one line that seemed to be the key but just made no sense to him, *"If pickles are your pleasure."* "Pickles, pickles, pickles. Why pickles?"

He abruptly realized he was working on a riddle that did not matter if he solved it or not, because the hiding place did not exist anymore.

"I need to get a fire going and my gear up to the loft before it gets dark," Asher reminded himself. "Pickles are your pleasure, just nonsense."

Asher rolled one massive stone after the other from the foundation wall to a safe distance away from the barn. He cleared the dry vegetation down to the damp soil and then arranged the boulders into a large ring. He knew his next move needed to be collecting firewood before nightfall. Asher has had experience trying to find dry twigs and branches to burn after dark with a flashlight. It is not an easy task.

He had noticed a stand of pines not far away and thought that this would be his best bet for dry wood. The bottom branches of pine trees die as the tree grows but stay attached to the tree. The dead branches are held off the ground, where the air can surround them, creating a natural store of dry material to burn.

Asher returned to his fire pit with as many branches as he could carry and then headed back for more. On his return trip he scored a whole scotch pine tree that had toppled over earlier that year. It was dead and dry but had not yet started to decay. It was only the size of a large Christmas tree so Asher was able to drag the whole thing back to camp.

Asher flicked his new lighter igniting the small pile of pine needles that he had placed in the center of the pit like a bullseye. The familiar scent of burning pine wafted lazily upward drifting and spreading in the stillness of the evening air. Asher placed tiny twigs on the bundle of needles and then larger and larger branches in a teepee configuration. In moments the fire roared and filled the fire ring.

Asher had packed one change of clothes and thankfully they were still dry. He stripped his damp clothes off and dressed in the dry ones from his pack. He hung his damp clothes on some branches of a tree that was far enough away from the fire that hopefully they would not ignite. Asher rolled one more boulder over to the side of the fire ring and sat on it.

Chapter 15

The Root Cellar

He sat by the fire eating two of the, by now, quite smooshed peanut butter and jam sandwiches. He watched the steam roll off his drying clothes and mix with the smoke of the campfire as he contemplated the day's events.

He ticked the events off in his head.

"Shotgun blasts almost deafens me."

"Too close of an encounter with a bear."

"Fell down a well."

"Found some coins."

"Found a key and riddle to treasure that can't be found."

"Pickles are your pleasure. Pickles are your pleasure. Pickles are your pleasure. Pickles are put in a jar. Maybe the treasure was in a jar," Asher mused.

Pickles were homemade back then for sure. They would have been kept in the basement on shelves with the other canned vegetables. Whatever it was, it was probably down in the basement of the old farm house.

"Probably in the root cellar," Asher reasoned to himself.

"The root cellar. The root cellar!" Asher exclaimed.

He suddenly realized that a hundred years ago the root cellar would not be in the house basement, it would be an actual root cellar. It would be a space dug out of the side of a hill on its own. Basically an underground room that used the natural underground constant temperature to store food. It kept the food stores cool in the summer and thawed during the winter. It would be a perfect place to hide something valuable.

Asher's eyes widened and pulse quickened as it dawned on him that the root cellar was likely still here and still intact. He jumped up and grabbed the flashlight.

He clicked the flashlight on and directed the beam horizontally, panning it three hundred and sixty degrees around where he stood. The flashlight beam fell on a rise in the landscape not far from his fire ring. Asher strode over to investigate. He studied the hill in front of him and settled on a flat spot on the east side. He reasoned that there could be a door buried there, somewhere under the decades of mulch and undergrowth.

Holding the flashlight in one hand he began to paw at the flattened area. The progress was slow so he went to retrieve the short round pointed shovel that he had brought. Asher stabbed at the earth with the shovel again and again, pulling the decayed undergrowth down and away.

Thunk. The shovel struck something solid and hollow. He drew back and thrust the shovel again. Again he heard the hollow thunk of shovel against wood protecting a void. Asher dropped to his knees and pulled the mulch away with his hands.

"A door!" Asher exclaimed.

Asher pawed at the plank door trying to clear all the debris from the framework. Finally, the complete door was exposed. It looked heavy and solid but too small. It was only half the height and width of a regular size door. The door hung on two immense hinges and donned a wrought iron latch scaled with decades of rust. The root cellar door had no lock, just the simple latch, and Asher, with some effort, abruptly unlatched it.

He slowly swung the door inward shining his flashlight to illuminate the cavity beyond. The heavy plank door creaked eerily, like entering a haunted house. In the gloom of the of the flashlight beam, Asher could make out rows of shelves, exactly like he would expect to see in a root cellar. The air was musty and earthy, smelling of mushrooms and mold. He cautiously stepped into the cramped space.

On the floor there was what was left of crates of potatoes, dried and shriveled like gigantic raisins. The shelves were lined with a plethora of various jars, mostly broken from the freezing and thawing of the seasons. The jar's contents were now reduced to lumps of browns, and grays, and greens, slumped on the shelves like melted scoops of ice cream.

Asher stood slightly stooped to accommodate the low ceiling as he aimed the flashlight beam along the shelving and to the back wall. He scanned the interior of the space without moving, trying to get his bearings.

The deafening silence of the hillside vault was abruptly invaded by an echoing scratching noise, or was it scurrying? Asher gasped slightly from the unexpected noise that seemed to come from inside the room with him. The acoustics of the root cellar made it impossible to tell where the sound was coming from.

Asher furiously washed the beam of the flashlight around the room jumping from corner, to corner, to ceiling, to floor, and back, desperately trying to locate the source of the noise. Scratch, scratch... or was it scurry?

Asher thought he caught a glimpse of movement on the shelf next to his head. He swung the flashlight beam around just in time to see the biggest rat he had ever laid eyes on flop down off the upper shelf to the one below. The slug of coarse black fur and naked tail repeated the movement to the next lower shelf and then again, until it arrived at the cellar floor.

Asher watched, froze in place, as he kept the light trained on the rodent. It crouched only inches from Asher's feet now. It was the size of a house cat and looked to be a formidable opponent for one too.

The rat paused then stood up on his hind legs with paws in front of him. His nose twitched as he sniffed the air and Asher could not help think of how much he looked like a miniature Jumbo.

The goliath rodent dropped back down to all fours then hurriedly waddled toward Asher, trekking right between his legs and out the door into the night. Asher was not particularly scared of rats but this one seemed just a little too tame and twice as big as it should be.

With the root cellar rat out of the way, Asher turned his attention to the rows of plank storage shelves.

"Pickles. Pickles. Pickles." Asher searched each shelf, each unbroken jar, trying to distinguish pickled cucumbers from the rest of the jars of decayed food. On the far end, on the left, on the bottom shelf, in a pint jar, there was what looked like pickled cucumbers… maybe.

He held up the cloudy jar illuminating it with the flashlight beam. It did indeed look like the greenish brown contents may have once been pickles. Asher shown the light on the shelves where he found the pickles and studied the space. There was no door and no knot. He did not even see a rope.

Asher panned the light all around the vicinity of the jars looking for anything that might pass as a door. And then he spotted it. On the back wall to the left of the suspect pickle jars hung a small square door closed tight with age. It was shrouded in a layer of dust and cobwebs and Asher used his hand to brush it clear. As dirt and grime fell away a heavily corroded brass keyhole revealed itself.

Asher quickly remembered the key and raced out of the root cellar, back to the campsite to retrieve the recently found box. He was back in an instant with the key and riddle engraved box cover. He knelt down and slid the skeleton key into the keyhole and turned it.

The key only turned a quarter turn but would not rotate any further. Asher worked the key back and forth jiggling and turning at the same time. It was no use. The lock was seized in place, refusing to unlock after maybe a hundred years of holding steadfast. He pulled the key out and sat on the ground in front of the little door, keeping it spotlighted with the flashlight beam.

He had gotten this close, he was not about to let this lock get between him and what was behind that door. He thought about what his next move should be.

"The pickaxe!" Asher whispered out loud excitedly.

He jumped up and was out the cellar door in a flash and returned just as quickly, lugging the heavy pointed implement. He propped the flashlight on a lower shelf and aimed it at the target. With both hands on the handle, Asher swung the pickaxe up and around over his right shoulder, taking aim at the rusted hinges that held the little door in place.

"Little door, meet the persuader," Asher murmured as he swung the pickaxe down and out, connecting with one of the hinges.

The hinge popped apart at the pin with a loud snap. He drew back and swung again hitting his mark. The second hinge popped like the first and there was nothing but the warped wood holding the door closed now. He swung the pickaxe again, harder this time, and the point penetrated right through the door.

One more swing and the point drove through and stuck fast into the door's deteriorating lumber, just as Asher hoped it would. He gripped the handle tightly and yanked hard. The little square door moved, just a little. He braced his feet against the wall for leverage and hauled on the pickaxe as hard as he could. Suddenly the door released itself from its century old position.

Asher flew backward landing flat on his back with a thump, still gripping the pickaxe. The little square door lay in two pieces at his feet. He fell hard enough that the concussion knocked the wind out of him. It took a few moments for him to catch his breath.

Asher sat up slowly, to look at the door. He realized the door was not there anymore. He first had thought the pickaxe had just pulled free. He sprang to his feet grabbing the flashlight off the shelf.

The flashlight beam quivered as Asher's hand shook a little in anticipation. The light flooded the void in the wall illuminating a neat row of pint Mason jars... empty Mason jars. There were seven empty jars donning the rusted remnants of lid rings, lined up in a row... and nothing else.

It was a small space and there was no way Asher had missed anything. There was just nothing in the tiny cupboard. Asher's heart sank. Whatever was in those jars someone had already beaten him to it. He turned to face the shelves and retrieved the key and box lid, then shown the light beam back to the space where the treasure was supposed to be.

He stared for a long moment at the void in the wall, then moved the box lid into the light. He read the riddle again. *It's not the one you think. Find the knot the key fits in...* "There is no knot. There's not even any rope." Asher mumbled to himself with exasperation.

He returned his attention back to the small cupboard where the Mason jars were lined up like a row of sentries guarding... what? Asher picked up an empty jar, rubbed the dust off, and then peered through the clear glass. There was nothing in it. He removed each jar and inspected them closely hoping he might find something. He was not willing to except there was nothing to be found after he had gotten this far.

As he picked up the final jar, Asher noticed a large blemish in the back board of the cupboard. It looked out of place because the back of the cupboard appeared to be made from clear pine except for this spot. He brushed at it with his hand until a large pine knot was revealed.

"Not a rope knot, a pine knot!" Asher exclaimed with sudden comprehension.

He scraped the years of dirt off the pine knot using his thumbnail exposing what he knew he would find. There, in the very center of the knot, was an irregular shaped hole, like a key hole. Asher immediately plunged his hand in his pocket and retrieved the skeleton key.

He slid the key into the center of the pine knot keeping the flashlight beam trained on the back of the recessed cabinet. The key slid in the hole almost half its length until it bumped what felt like a metallic stop. Asher turned the key counterclockwise one half turn easily and then felt a click.

The skeleton key fit the lock hidden behind the pine knot perfectly and this lock did not seem to be corroded. As soon as the lock clicked, the back of the little cupboard popped forward and then sat slightly ajar, revealing the false back.

Asher reached in his pocket for his Case pocket knife, locked open the blade, and slid it in the crevasse between the false back and the cupboard's shelf. He twisted the knife working the false back open a little more. Now he could get his fingers behind it and he pulled the board forward.

Asher stood there, stooped down holding the false back in one hand and the flashlight in the other, contemplating the new void that was now exposed. Directly behind the false back was compacted grey clay dirt except for a carved out rectangle in the dead center. Asher moved his head and flashlight in close and peered into the tiny cubby hole. The hole seemed to be dug deep, maybe almost two feet into the earth.

Asher could see a glint reflecting the flashlight beam in the very back of the hollowed out space. It seemed to him this would be a perfect place to set a trap.

"Reach for the bait and slam, gotcha." Asher thought.

He studied the hole for a moment and then finally determined it was safe to reach his hand and arm in. Slowly and blindly he groped to the back of the hole until his fingers touched something smooth and cold. He reached in farther and grasped the cylinder shaped object pulling it back and out.

"Another jar?" Asher blurted out with exasperated disgust. "What is it with these jars?"

At least this jar had some weight to it, affirming it was not empty. The jar was shrouded with dust but the lid was not rusted. Asher scrubbed the jar on his shirt wiping it clean. He held in front of the light but he still could not see through the glass. It looked as if the interior of the jar had been painted black.

He gripped the lid and twisted but it would not budge. Using a corner of his shirt for a better grip, he again gripped and twisted on the lid with as much effort as he could summon. The lid broke free.

Asher finished unscrewing the lid and dropped it to the ground. A yellowed folded slip of paper greeted him as he shown the light in. And beyond the fold of paper… was gold dust. Asher's heart stopped and then resumed, at twice the rate.

His eyes wide, he plucked the paper out and then gave the jar a little shake to see the dust jump a bit. He tipped the mouth of the jar to his open palm and shook it. The gold dust jumped and tumbled down the wall of the container until a small amount arrived to his open hand.

"Gold for sure!" Asher whispered with almost uncontained excitement as he moved his thumb through the shimmering coarse dust.

He carefully tipped his palm back to the mouth of the jar, returning the precious gold granules to the blacked out glass container. He used his thumb to assure every bit was replaced. He shook the jar lightly again as he peered in. It looked as though there was only about a half an inch of gold dust in the bottom of the jar. Asher thought maybe this amounted to about two ounces, but he was not sure.

He turned his attention to the yellowed fold of paper. The paper was thick and stiff as he gingerly peeled it open. The musty smell of it reminded Asher of his grandparent's encyclopedias. As he opened it, the paper split at the folds creating a tattered jigsaw puzzle of a note. He laid it out on one of the shelves beside him trying to keep the ripped squares of paper in place.

The ink was faded to a pale gray but mostly still legible. Asher squinted in the low light at the faded words and read aloud.

Dear Grandpa,
I am in some serious trouble. I need to borrow some of the gold dust that you have hidden here. I have weighed out what I took so I know how much to pay you back. I am borrowing eighty ounces. I will you pay you back very soon. I am so sorry about taking this without asking you but I have no choice. I will explain it to you someday.
Again, sorry.
Love,
A. M.

"A. M. obviously never paid back the gold," Asher thought to himself, "eighty ounces, wow! The jar must have been filled to the top with that much gold."

Asher looked at the couple of ounces still left in the bottom of the jar.

"It was better than nothing," Asher reasoned.

He held the jar up to the flashlight beam and shook the contents once more watching it shimmer and refract the light. He sighed with some disappointment as he thought about how much gold could have been in that jar. Tomorrow he would trek to the cave. Maybe he would find more gold there than he could spend.

Chapter 16

Sleeping Under the Stars

With flashlight in one hand, and the jar of gold in the other, he returned to the camp fire. He sat there thinking about the day's events wondering what tomorrow would bring. "Two ounces of gold is worth twelve hundred dollars. Not a fortune, but a lot of money." Asher thought with mild satisfaction. "Maybe tomorrow I'll find a fortune."

The camp fire snapped and sparked and began to fade. Asher was fading fast too, and he soon decided to retire to bed. He removed the rope from his backpack and threw one end up to the loft. Then he tied the other end to the strap on his pack preparing to haul it up.

Asher once again scaled the supporting post up to the loft. Finding the end of the rope, he threaded it through the massive pulley and began to pull on it. Hand over hand he heaved the rope through the pulley, dragging his pack up toward him, inch by inch. When the pack arrived at the pulley, Asher tied off the rope and retrieved it. He untied his sleeping bag from the outside of the pack and unrolled it.

Asher spread the sleeping bag out on the loft floor well away from the edge. He had been known to toss and turn quite a bit in his sleep and did not want to end up falling to the ground before the night was over.

The night air was clean, and clear, and cold. Asher climbed in his sleeping bag tucking himself in all but his face against the frigid night air. He lay safely up in the loft gazing at the stars and crescent moon, feeling good about how the day had played out.

The inky blackness of the endless sky twinkled with countless pricks of light all competing for Asher's gaze. He found the northern star, and the big dipper, and then the little dipper. These were constellations his big brother had pointed out to him long ago on a moonlight downhill sledding excursion.

Asher and his brother finally had tired of trudging through thigh high snow to the top of the sliding hill behind their house. They had laid on their backs at the bottom of the hill, red plastic sleds between them and the snow, staring up at the impossible bigness, and blackness, and brightness of the fresh winter sky. The two brother's breath billowed from their mouths as their young lungs strained against the sharp cold.

They had laid there, head to head discussing parents, and Christmas, and friends, and life, and death, and all of the other things only children, only brothers, could talk about. Asher was very young then, only about five, but he remembered it now like it was only moments ago. What had happened between him and Adam?

"We grew up..." Asher supposed with a nostalgic sigh.

He closed his eyes and could still see the apparition of stars and moonlight floating behind his eyelids. He let his mind drift to gold dust, and Adeline, and what might be.

The crickets and a distant whippoorwill sang him gently asleep. The exhaustion of the day induced an almost coma-like sleep and Asher slept hard until early morning.

Just before dawn Asher's eyes flew open and he sat bolt upright. Maybe he had smelled him, or maybe it was the low quiet grunts, but Asher knew at once Jumbo was back. He wriggled out of his sleeping bag with as much speed and stealth he could manage. It sounded like Jumbo was directly below him sniffing and grunting like a truffle pig on the hunt.

Asher crept to the edge of the loft and cautiously peered down to the area just below the pulley and rope. Jumbo apparently had tracked the smell of the peanut butter emanating from Asher's backpack, and it led him directly to the loft. Asher was thankful he did not leave his pack down on the ground for Jumbo to maul. Now he hoped he was correct in believing Jumbo would not be able to scale the narrow supporting post.

Just as Asher leaned his head over the edge, Jumbo rose onto his hind legs, assuming his begging-dog pose once again. Asher abruptly jerked his head back out of Jumbo's line of site trying to stifle his panicked breathing. He rolled flat to his stomach and pressed his cheekbone to the floor of the loft squinting through a space between the planks. Asher watched the immense black bear through the crack in the floor, drop down to all four paws, poised in the direction of the post.

In one stride Jumbo was at the base of the post and back up on his hind legs reaching and stretching and clawing. His front paws hooked some of the barn boards but as he strained against them, they just splintered against the force. Jumbo sniffed and grunted as he clawed at the post, but it was no use. Much to Jumbos disappointment, he could not get up to the loft where he knew there was food to be had.

Asher laid motionless and silent as he watched Jumbo try in vain to claw his way up to the loft. There was more pawing, and scratching, and grunting, until Jumbo decided that he had exhausted every option. Asher let out a hushed sigh as Jumbo dropped back down to all fours and lumbered off, looking disappointed and defeated. Asher watched him disappear into the overgrown cedar hedges with relief and possibly a little lingering apprehension.

The sun hovered just below the tree line creating varied shades of an intense pink sunrise.

"Red sky at night, sailors delight. Red sky in the morning, sailors take warning." It was a prediction that Asher's father said often, and it usually proved true. Asher was likely in for a rain storm today.

He picked himself up off the loft floor and stood at the edge gazing at where Jumbo had wandered into the woods. His mind was racing with worries for the approaching day.

"Would Jumbo keep his distance today? Would the storm hold off until he reached the cave? Would he find anything in there?" Asher fretted to himself.

Asher could hear Uncle Jeb's voice creeping into his thoughts, "worrying never helped anything."

And so with Uncle Jeb's wisdom ringing in his ears, Asher attacked the day. He snatched his backpack up and retrieved the rest of the sandwiches. He ate two more for his breakfast and decided to leave the rest up in the loft. Asher was quite sure it was the peanut butter and jam sandwiches that were attracting the giant black bear and not the sealed candy bars. He also left his sleeping bag behind on the loft floor, rolled tightly, hoping to return that night to sleep.

He attached his pack to the rope that ran through the antique pulley and lowered it to the ground with a thud. Asher wanted to use the rope himself for an easier descent but reasoned he would need the rope to explore in the cave. So, he untied it from the beam where he had anchored it and tossed it to the ground. Once again he shimmied down the post with some difficulty and landed himself next to the pack.

Asher lashed the pickaxe and shovel to his pack and slung it over his shoulders. He pulled out his compass, determined a northwesterly bearing, and surveyed the route ahead. He glanced up at the gathering storm clouds with a faint feeling of dread.

"Maybe it will hold off until I get to the cave," Asher thought to himself hopefully.

Asher leaned slightly forward against the weight of the pack and began his march with an early morning determination and a sense of looming storm urgency. He bush-wacked a new trail in a due northwest course crashing through the impossibly thick undergrowth. He quickly punched through the dense brush and found himself streamside in under a half an hour.

Chapter 17

Timber Rattlesnake

Within minutes of traveling up Old Indian Creek, Asher realized he had landed exactly where he had hoped he would, almost to where the stream's branches joined. He could feel the elevation rise as he hiked with greater and greater effort. And there it was, the fork in the creek, where the east branch joined with the west. Asher paused as the two branches of the creek came into view. Uncle Jeb's words of warning now ran through his head.

"I hope you're wrong this time Uncle Jeb. I hope the west branch is good luck for me," Asher murmured as he tried to remember if he had ever known Uncle Jeb to be wrong.

He was still on the east side of the creek and needed to cross now. After a brief survey of the landscape, Asher chose a narrow stretch just ahead and bounded over to the other side using four stepping stones. Just as his foot touched the west bank of the creek, a damp gust of wind rushed into him, almost knocking him over. He was able to recover his balance with a few stutter steps.

The dark thunder heads drifted in from the west with too much eagerness. A deep, low rumble like war drums from the mountains beyond rolled across the woods carrying sprinkles that wet Asher's face. The air was heavy enough to drink. The storm was approaching.

Asher decided that he needed to cut down his hiking time in order to reach the cave before the brunt of the storm reached him. There was a sharp bend in the west branch that doubled back on itself. He had followed right along the creek on the way up and back but he thought he may be able to now cut that bend off completely. He had spotted a bare ridge high above the creek that looked as though it might be a faster trail to the cave.

As he approached the bend in the creek he began looking for an opening in the underbrush to start up towards the ridge. He cut off from the creek's bank through a break in the alders and was immediately greeted with impossibly steep terrain. Asher leaned hard against the incline, his feet slipping in the mulch and on the moss covered rocks. He dug and pawed further and further up, as he used saplings and an occasional jagged rock for hand holds.

Thirty feet up the steep grade Asher's effort was finally rewarded with a sudden break in vegetation. The brush gave way to bare rock and he scrambled up it to arrive at the very top of the ridge. He stood at the summit looking across the exposed rock spine. It was a straight shot down the bare ridge almost all the way to the cave. This natural path along the ridge is known as a hogs-back and it was exactly what Asher had hoped that he would find up there.

The humid wind gusted once more with the smell of rain and a noticeable descent in temperature. Now the rain drops were bigger and they pelted Asher's head and shoulders and the moss covered rock under his feet. He scouted a path in front of him and hurriedly began his hike across the ridge.

The bare rocky path became increasingly slick with every moment of rain, making it difficult for Asher to maintain a rapid pace. As he moved along the ridge he peered over the edge to his left and he estimated the drop to be more than fifty feet almost straight down.

The apex of the ridge was only about two feet wide in some places and almost coming to a point in others. He tried to hug the right side of the ridge as it looked little safer. The right side was still a good ten foot drop down to a ledge that jutted out from the rock face and then dropped away another twenty feet.

The rain was soaking through his shirt and running down his forehead into his eyes. Asher was sure he had only about fifteen or twenty minutes before he would reach the cave, but he would be thoroughly drenched by then. He tried to pick up the his pace.

He hopped to a jagged rock landing on a patch of moss he had tried to miss. His foot immediately slid down and to the side violently twisting his ankle. Asher cried out in pain as his ankle gave out and his leg crumpled. To his horror, he found himself falling forward toward the right side of the drop off. He tried to catch himself as he tumbled head first, but it was no use. He thrust his hands out in front of him just in time to absorb the brunt of the fall, but his momentum sealed his fate.

Asher rolled, shoulder first, over the right side of the cliff. He lingered in the air long enough to think about how much this was going to hurt as he plunged the more than ten feet to the ledge below. He landed with a bone jarring thud knocking the breath out of him.

Asher laid in a heap down on the cliff ledge for a long moment, gasping to catch his breath. He tried to breath in once, twice, three times and finally felt his lungs fill. As the breath returned to his lungs it was immediately followed by pain in his chest that seemed to spread through his whole body. His hands, his arms, his shoulder, but mostly his head throbbed with pain.

Still lying in the position that he had landed in, he reached his hand up to his forehead to where a sharp pain was stabbing him with every beat of his heart. He felt a large goose egg of a lump where his head had connected with a stone upon his impact. He pulled his hand away and looked at it. There was a smear of blood on his fingertips.

"That's not good," Asher murmured with a little alarm.

He rolled from his side to his back. His pack was still on but the shovel and pickaxe had come loose in the fall and now laid a few feet away. The roll to his back caused some pain but not enough for Asher to think anything was broken. The rain had abruptly stopped for now but it had done its damage. Asher had already slipped and fallen and the lichen covered rocks were now as slick as ice.

He slowly, very slowly, sat up and then moved his head from side to side. He lifted his right arm, bent it at the elbow like a wing, and rotated it at the shoulder. He then did the same with his left arm assessing the damage. Again, there was some pain but he seemed to have full range of motion. It was likely there was nothing broke.

He reached up and felt his head again. It was a huge lump but at least it was not bleeding badly. Asher shifted from his sitting position to his hands and knees preparing to stand up. He drew his right leg up under him and pushed propelling him to a standing position. There was more shooting pain in his back as he stood up. But this back pain, and all of the rest of his pain, was suddenly and terrifyingly forgotten.

As Asher arched his back in a standing stretch, he froze where he stood. He heard a noise he could not place, directly in front of him. The sound was not familiar to him from any conscious memory, but it resonated in him on a primal level. It was a warning sound programmed in his DNA. It was the ominous rattle of an apex predator.

There, coiled on the bare rock, superbly camouflaged, not more than four feet from where Asher stood, was a monstrous timber rattlesnake. His inky black eyes were set narrowly in a wide wedge of a head. It had armor looking scales that covered a thick body that was coiled on itself.

Asher had read about them in an Adirondack guide book that E. B. Marley sold to its scant few tourist customers. He had never actually seen a timber rattlesnake. For that matter he had never even heard of anyone coming across one, but the guide book had said that they could be found in that area.

Nothing puts a situation in perspective like being faced with possible death. A bite from this snake would be lethal unless treated with anti-venom. Asher was too far out in the wilderness to ever make it back to civilization for help. He absolutely could not get bit by this snake. His mind raced with these thoughts as he simultaneously tried to recall the information he had read about timber rattlesnakes. There bite is lethal, they can sense body heat, they usually do not strike unless provoked, they have a strike range of over three feet.

"Am I four feet away? Maybe not quite." Asher speculated.

Still froze in position he gingerly, so gingerly, moved his right leg back and away from the rattlesnake, letting the rest of his body follow as fluidly as possible. He took one more slow, cautious step back, retreating from the snake's strike zone. Asher finally exhaled for the first time after seeing the timber rattlesnake.

He glanced behind him and then beyond where the snake lay coiled, assessing his predicament. Behind him the ledge faded into the cliff face, leaving no escape route in that direction. Beyond the snake, the ledge actually widened and progressed up the cliff face, providing a possible route back to the ridge.

The snake once again rattled its foreboding tail while constantly flicking its forked tongue, tasting saturated summer air, sensing the massive threatening heat signature in his path. Asher somehow had to get by this snake.

He glanced around again and spotted a broken branch just behind him. That was just what Asher was hoping to find. With his eyes locked on the snake's unblinking eyes, he crouched at a glacial pace to retrieve the branch. He felt behind him with his left hand never taking his eyes of the snake. His hand groped blindly until it finally came to rest on the branch and he grasped it.

As he moved the branch around in front of him, he also stood up with slow deliberation. The branch was only about two feet long. This was well within the strike range and Asher was not sure what his next move would be. The timber rattlesnake decided for him.

With lightning speed, the rattlesnake struck towards Asher. At the very same moment, Asher reacted with instinctual reflex swinging the branch as hard as he could at the snake. Asher caught the rattler just behind the head and it sent the snake flying off the ledge dropping like a length of fire hose twenty feet below. As he watched it flailing in the air he could see the enormity of the snake and he estimated it was almost six feet long. It landed with a thud below and then slithered for cover.

"A rare encounter with a deadly rattlesnake is not exactly good luck," Asher thought to himself with apprehension.

With the deadly snake out of the way, Asher resumed taking stock of his injuries. Besides the bump on his head, it looked as though he just had some scrapes and bruises. His head was still throbbing but not bleeding anymore. He looked ahead to where the ledge widened. It was the only way back up to the ridge. He collected his pickaxe and shovel, lashed them once again to his pack, and moved forward.

He moved slowly along the ledge not wanting to repeat his fall. As he inched his way along, he studied the cliff face and finally came to rest at an area riddled with deep cracks. He looked up the rock face to the ridge overhead and estimated it was only about an eight-foot climb.   He knew the cracks and crevices would make perfect hand and foot holds to free climb back up to the ridge.

He checked to make sure the shovel and pickaxe were secured to his pack and began his ascent. He reached high over his head and found a solid hand hold. As he pulled against his body weight, he was abruptly reminded of his fall with a shooting pain in his shoulder. Asher knew this was no time to wimp out. He ignored the pain and pulled hard to hoist himself to the next hand hold. His left hand found another good hand hold as his right foot followed up to another divot in the rock.

He pulled with his arms and pushed with his legs, reaching, grasping, stepping, and then he was back up on the bare spine of the ridge. He lay there for a moment, panting as he became aware of the pain from the bruises and abrasions again. He could feel the shovel and pickaxe drive into his back through the pack. The rain was falling again, pelting his face and drenching him once more.

As he laid there, a memory of complete exhaustion drifted into his mind. It was two years ago, and he was laying in the snow, flat on his back, drenched to the skin with maple sap and melted spring snow. His body was aching from gathering sap all day, for the fifth day in a row. His hands and feet were freezing but, at the same time, his body was overheated.

He had fallen down for the hundredth time as he tried to carry the five-gallon white plastic pails full of maple sap through the thigh high snow. The maple sap that he had been desperately trying to carry to the gathering tub on the horse drawn sleigh had once again dumped all over him. Asher had laid in the snow, completely exhausted, muscles aching, feet and hands numb with cold, miserable, and on the verge of tears.

Of course in this setting, crying was not an option. For that matter, laying in the snow feeling sorry for yourself was not an option either. It was an unspoken code among men working together, doing anything physical. Whether it was logging, or building, or gathering sap for maple syrup production, you pulled your weight and did not complain. On the contrary, the goal was to work harder, be faster, and be tougher than the next guy without complaint. If you could bleed and grin about it, that was all the better.

It did not matter that Asher was only twelve at the time. The code applied to him because he was part of the team gathering sap. What sap Asher did not gather; someone else would have to. He had known that quitting before the sap was gathered was not an option.

The neighbor who had asked Asher to help out in his sugarbush during winter break yelled out to him.

"Are you okay?" the neighbor had asked in gruff voice.

Asher knew that this question really meant, "do you have any broken bones?" because that would be the only excuse to stop working.

"Yup!" Asher had answered with as much bravado as he could summon.

"Well get up then. The sap's not gonna gather itself," the neighbor had shot back.

The neighbor's words now rang in Asher's ears. The sap would not gather itself and no one would find the gold for him. Time to get up and man up.

Asher rocked to his feet awkwardly with a grunt. There was a flash of lightning that was followed to close by a clap of thunder. It was now dawning on Asher just how much danger he was in. The last place anyone should be in a thunder and lightning storm is at the top of a bare ridge. He had inadvertently made himself a human lightning rod.

The lightning flashed again and the crack of thunder was even closer behind it. Light travels faster than sound and Asher knew that the closer the lightning and thunder came together, the closer the storm was. The storm was upon him. He pointed himself towards the cave, put his head down, and resumed his trudging hike.

He took one measured step after the other, quickly but carefully placing each foot, one in front of the other. He glanced up once in a while to be sure he was still trekking in the direction of the cave. He was close now.

Just as he glanced up to get his bearings again, a furious tongue of lightning struck the mountain ahead of him, accompanied with a simultaneous blast of thunder. Asher jumped back and gasped. He was breathing violently, almost hyperventilating.

"That was too close," Asher whispered as he desperately tried to calm his breathing. "Way too close."

He peered through the haze of the driving rain, trying to decide exactly where he needed to go next. Finally, he spotted a glimpse of Old Indian Creek and began his descent toward it. It was a steep grade no matter which path he picked. He now was back among the thick underbrush and the slippery black mud.

Asher worked his way down until he came to a bare boulder the size of a house jutting from the side of the hill and ending in a sort of pool that was fed by Old Indian Creek. He considered his options for a moment until another flash of lightning and clap of thunder interrupted his thought. The crash of lightning inspired him to pick the quickest way down.

He tossed his pack to the poolside below just missing the water. He then sat on the smooth, rain soaked boulder, leaned back, closed his eyes, held his breath, and gave himself a shove with his hands. He slid a few feet on the bare rock then was falling through the air. He landed in the pool with a tremendous splash. It was thankfully deep and Asher plunged to the bottom, feet first, then immediately popped back up to the surface. He bobbed there like a cork until he oriented himself and then breast stroked to shore.

He dragged himself from the cold water and rested beside his pack. He had immediately recognized the pool when he saw it standing up on the boulder. Asher realized he was only a five-minute hike to the mouth of the cave.

"Finally!" Asher exclaimed aloud.

He suddenly was recharged with anticipation as he stood up and then started upstream to the cave entrance. As he hiked the last few minutes of the journey to the head of the creek, the rainfall lightened a little along with Asher's mood. This trip had turned out to be much more difficult than it should have been.

Chapter 18

Back In The Cave

Asher stood in the middle of Old Indian Creek, staring at its source, soaked, bruised, scraped, exhausted, but not defeated. Not even close. He slung his pack off his shoulders and approached the sideways mouth of the cave. It seemed to be frowning at him like one of those murderous clown pictures with the sharp teeth. Asher shuddered a little.

"Cursed. Bad luck," Uncle Jeb's and Claudie's words rattled in his head.

"I don't know about this cave, but the trip up here was no picnic," Asher mused to himself.

"Well, nothing ventured, nothing gained." Asher recalled a customer at the hardware store had said.

He pulled out his brother's flashlight and wiped the rain off of it as well as he could. He unscrewed the top and poured the old batteries into his pack then replaced them with the fresh set he had brought. He shown the light into the dubious opening. It looked smaller than he had remembered it. Still shining the flashlight through the opening he wedged his backpack in as far as he could reach and dropped it.

A crow cawed in a nearby birch tree as Asher contorted his body to fit the jagged opening. He cautiously inched his way in. Thunder rolled outside as the cave consumed him. At least Asher thought it was thunder, or possibly it was something else. It did not sound exactly like thunder, but more like a low howling, more like groans maybe. Asher was now in the cave and stood.

He threw his pack over one shoulder with the shovel and pickaxe dangling to one side. The cave looked different to him now with the brand new flashlight batteries illuminating the cavernous space. Asher panned the light from side to side, sweeping the interior with its beam. The space seemed much bigger than when he was here the first time.

Asher's plan was to follow the stream up into the cave for as far as he could while searching for any signs of gold. If he did not find any nuggets laying in the creek or gold veins in the walls of the cave, he would then pan for gold as he worked his way back.

Claudie had mentioned that Ansylum had found a massive gold vein before he got trapped in here. Usually Asher would not put much stock in anything that Claudie said, but this was something Asher had to check out. Claudie had said that Ansylum had found the gold vein down a narrow shaft.

He flicked the beam around him once more then shown it down by his feet and began to pick his way upstream. Bent over, meticulously moving the flashlight beam over the water at his feet he was reminded of picking up night crawlers on warm spring nights. Of course a gold nugget was worth much more than a three cent fish worm.

He tossed his pack onto a large boulder that jutted up from the stream as he continued his search in the creek. The shovel and pickaxe landed with an echoing clank, and something else. The sound was too loud to be just from the shovel clanging on the rock. It echoed, and echoed, and echoed, to the point Asher stopped searching and held his breath to listen.

"This place has some strange acoustics," Asher thought to himself and then resumed his search.

As he moved the flashlight back and forth over the stream bed, Asher thought he glimpsed a shimmer in the water. He peered intensely through the rippling water. The object was definitely reflecting the light. He used his finger to pick at the shimmering object. Sure enough, it was a gold nugget. This nugget was even bigger than the first one he had found.

Asher plucked it from the stream and carefully placed it in the palm of his left hand. He held it out in front of him marveling at the shimmering pebble he had just found.

"There really is more gold in this cave," Asher murmured excitedly.

He pocketed it and continued prospecting upstream. He directed the flashlight beam ahead of him trying to determine the size of the cave. The beam faded to an indeterminate end, suggesting the enormity of the space. Asher now realized the cave was definitely much larger than he had originally thought.

As he took another step upstream, Asher heard the rumble of thunder again, and what sounded like pebbles falling into the water behind him. He swung the flashlight around in time to see ripples in the water but nothing more.

"Was that thunder?" Asher whispered.

He directed the light overhead to study the ceiling of the cave. It sparkled with moisture and was rough with erosion but it looked solid. There did not seem to be loose debris on the ceiling that could fall into the water.

"What could have fallen in the water?" Asher asked himself

Asher shrugged it off and continued his search for more gold. He moved slowly, deliberately, carefully, intently, deeper and deeper into the cave. He suddenly stopped short. He thought he heard a faint tapping somewhere deep in the cave. He held his breath, froze in place, listening for what he thought he had heard.

Tap… tap… tap… tap. It was a muffled cadence, almost whisper. Was it ahead of him or behind him? Was it even there at all? He panned the flashlight beam all around him illuminating the walls, and ceiling, and water by his feet, but not the cavernous space ahead of him. His light faded to nothing out there.

He continued to hold his breath until he was sure he could not hear the eerie tapping anymore. He exhaled slowly and almost silently. His heart thumped high in his chest.

"Nothing," Asher whispered trying to convince himself.

A feeling of sadness was creeping over Asher as he resumed his hunt for gold. Actually not quite sadness but more like dread, or maybe grief. There was a glint in the water ripples to the right of where he stood. The glint pushed the melancholy feeling away for the moment.

Asher took a step and then plunged his hand in the cold mountain stream harvesting yet another gold nugget. He held it between his thumb and fore finger rolling it this way and that, watching the light from the flashlight dance around it. This nugget was the size of a quarter, and spherical, and weighty.

His eyes were wide, and glazed, and unblinking, as the fever rose in him, gripped him, consumed him. Any fear he had a moment ago was gone now, along with any pain from injuries, and possibly, any good sense. Asher was possessed with the hunt for more gold.

"Time to go search for Ansylum's gold vein," Asher said loud enough for anyone or anything that might be in that cave to hear.

He pointed the flashlight straight upstream and followed the beam into the blackness. Asher trudged up the stream splashing through the water, not even trying to hop from stone to stone. He was on a mission now to find where the cave narrowed to a shaft.

The flashlight bobbed and darted in front of him as he awkwardly stumbled ever deeper in the cave. He finally slowed when the flashlight beam began flicking on the walls ahead of him indicating the space was shrinking.

Somewhere in the darkness over his splashing and trudging, Asher heard the tap… tap… again. He suddenly halted his every movement and stood frozen and breathless. There it was again, tap… tap…tap… or rather tink… tink…tink… like metal on stone. It was louder this time, but still just above a whisper. Tink… tink… It echoed in the in the cavernous space and sounded as if it was coming from all directions.

Asher exhaled slowly, tink… tink… It sounded almost like a shovel clanging against rock, or a pickaxe. Was someone else in here with him? No one knew he was coming here. No one knew what he had found. No one knows about this cave. Tink… tink… tink… It was louder, then faded to nothing.

"Nothing," Asher whispered.

He strained to listen as he held his breath again. There was just the deafening silence broke only by the faint trickling of water. He slowly shown the flashlight beam up, then down, then side to side.

"Nothing," Asher whispered again.

Shining the light down by his feet once more, he began again to hike upstream. This time he moved slightly more guarded. The unsettling and unknown noise seemed to have quenched his fever a little.

The flashlight's intensity was already starting to wane and Asher could only see a few feet in front of him. He hopped up on a smooth stone and peered ahead in the gloom. He thought he could see the end of the cave in the muted light. He hopped one more stone, and then another, and another, and then came face to face with a rock wall. The creek by his feet disappeared into the ground.

He now stood at the source of the west branch of Old Indian Creek. The source was a spring that bubbled out of the ground deep in a cave on the top of a weather worn mountain. Asher felt some satisfaction in the fact that he had found the source of the west branch of Old Indian

Creek. He supposed that not many people had ever stood here.

Chapter 19

Ansylum

Tink… tink… tink… The sound returned as a distant echo all around Asher. He swung the light around to his left, to the only open space from where he stood. The flashlight beam traced the wall opposite him. As it did, it disappeared for a moment then reappeared. The flashlight beam must have cast into a hollow in the cave wall. The unsettling sound now melted to nothing again.

Asher moved to the cave wall to investigate the space his light had disappeared into. There, at waist level, there was an opening in the wall about two feet across and three feet tall. It was jagged and irregular and definitely natural, definitely not man made.

Asher peered in and extended his arm that held the flashlight into the blackness of the newly discovered cavern. A narrow cavern… like a shaft…

"This must be it! The shaft Ansylum found!" Asher said aloud with amazement.

Just as he said this, the flashlight dimmed, and then flickered, and then dimmed out. Asher pounded the head of the flashlight against his left hand in a furious panic. It blinked back on and then held a steady beam. Asher exhaled a loud with a long sigh of relief but the panic of complete blackness was still caught in his throat.

Asher was suddenly aware of a very important detail he had overlooked. He only had one flashlight. No backup. If this light went out, he may not ever be able to find his way out of the cave.

"How could I be so stupid?" Asher scolded himself. "I don't even have any more batteries. How could I have overlooked that?"

He thought about shutting the flashlight off to conserve what batteries he had left, but he could not bring himself to do it. It was not that Asher was afraid of the dark but this place had him rattled.

What sounded like thunder rolled again, somewhere beyond the cave. As it did Asher thought he felt a slight tremor in the rock beneath his feet.

"That's really weird," Asher whispered worriedly. "This place must be getting to me."

Asher was burning battery life and he knew he had to make a move. Leading with his flashlight beam he ducked his head and stepped up and in, to enter the shaft. It was cramped but not an impossible fit. He slowly inched his way into what he hoped would turn out to be Ansylum's gold vein shaft.

He contorted his body this way and that, awkwardly crawling and shimmying his way deeper and deeper. He could not hold the light out in front of him as he maneuvered down the shaft, so he reluctantly flipped the flashlight off and felt his way along.

The air was even heavier in this cramped space and the musty decayed smell was almost overpowering. Suddenly Asher could smell another odor blending with the moist decayed smell. It was, impossibly, the smell of tobacco, pipe tobacco.

The unmistakable smell of pipe tobacco stopped Asher cold. This odor did not belong here, and it unnerved him more than anything else in the cave had so far. Noises, and even perceived movement, could be explained away, but not this smell. Asher breathed deep and exhaled. It smelled like Uncle Jeb's pipe tobacco, there was no question about it.

He paused there in the dark recess of the cave shaft for a long moment, trying to process the mishmash of odors. He wriggled his hand from down by his thigh to out in front of him and flipped the light back on. It flickered then held a steady beam. He washed the flashlight beam over the ragged interior of the of the shaft.

The space was narrowing and seemed to close completely just a few feet ahead. Keeping the flashlight on and pointed ahead of him, Asher maneuvered ahead another few inches. His heart was pounding and he was breathing heavy. Tink… tink…

The sound seemed close and distant at the same time. It echoed from behind him, and before him, and even from the walls around him. Tink… tink…

"What *is* that?" Asher asked with exasperation.

He shined the light all around him in desperation. He could see nothing that would cause the noise. What he *did* see was a flit of refraction on the wall just ahead of him to his right. He pulled himself forward for a closer look… and there it was. A six-inch-wide gold vein imbedded in a deposit of quartz that ran parallel and away into the shadows. An unbelievable amount of gold.

It glimmered, and reflected, and sparkled, and glowed, in the gloom of the cave's shaft. It was a pirate's treasure of gold, a king's ransom of gold, a national treasure of gold. It was an impossible amount of gold, millions of dollars of gold. And it lay inches from Asher's face imbedded in the rock.

Asher traced the vein away from him with the beam of light to where the vein ran into a pile of rubble that blocked the shaft. It was just as Claudie had described.

"Who knows how long this vein is," Asher thought to himself with optimistic excitement.

Asher was wishing he would have somehow dragged the pickaxe along with him down the shaft. There was no way he was going to be able to extract any of this gold without it. He would have to go back and retrieve the pickaxe and shovel if he were to have any chance of harvesting this gold. Before he headed back to get his equipment, Asher decided he would see if he could unearth any more of the gold vein by hand.

He worked his way to the end of the shaft where the loose rubble laid and began digging at it with his bare hands. He moved small boulders and coarse sand away from the gold vein. As he revealed more and more gold his effort became frantic. He stuffed the rocky debris behind him and beside him. He was running out of room to excavate.

He grasped a large stone and pulled it toward him. As he removed the stone, he exposed more gold, and something else. It was a piece of leather. Asher brushed away more sand and then inspected the thing that should not be there. He moved in close, bathing the tattered leather in the flashlight beam. It was not just a piece of leather, but it was what looked like what had been an old glove.

"Maybe Ansylum had lost this glove here when he found the gold vein," Asher speculated to himself.

The glove was almost completely exposed now and Asher grasped the ragged fingers and gave it a tug. The glove came loose and Asher now held it in his hand, scrutinizing it. As he studied the partially decayed glove something caught his eye in the debris where he had pulled it from. He trained the light on it.

It was a pale yellow object, almost the color of old parchment paper. It was not like the surrounding pinkish and off-white color of the sand and stones. It was cylindrical with a knob on each end and about half the size of a Crayola crayon. Asher brushed at it with his fingertips. As he did, he exposed another of these objects, and then another. They were bones. Asher was sure of it.

"Some animal must have died down here," Asher reasoned as he almost forgot about the fortune of gold that hung in the rock just over his head.

He pawed at the tiny bones unearthing more. He wanted to determine what kind of animal would have crawled way down in this cavern. He excavated more small bones, and then, two long bones appeared out of the sand. Very long bones. The bones were as long as Asher's forearm.

He stared at the two long bones he had found for a long moment. As he did, a sick, tightening feeling crept into the pit of his stomach. These were not animal bones... They were human bones... a human arm and hand.

Asher's chest tightened like a vise. Tink... tink... He moved away from the bones in a slow backwards crawl, all the while he kept the human remains spotlighted. Tink... tink... What *was* that creepy noise?

Asher's gold fever was rapidly draining from his veins and was now being replaced by an icy fear. The deep roll of thunder rumbled and echoed through the cavernous cave and down the shaft where Asher lay. A shivering jolt ran the length of Asher's spine up into his tensed neck. Tink... Tink...

The flashlight blinked, then dimmed, then faded out. Asher frantically banged the flashlight on his opposite forearm, trying to will the light to return. It did not. With the light out, and suddenly plunged into complete darkness, Asher was thoroughly and completely panicked.

Asher balled his whole body up, and then flipped around in the shaft to retreat. In the inky blackness, he groped his way along the shaft back to the main cave. In what seemed like forever but was only a few minutes, he finally reached the end of the shaft and tumbled back into the gaping cave.

He furiously shook the flashlight, flipping it on and off, finally it blinked on, dimly. Asher breathed out a hard, loud sigh of relief and then consciously tried to control his panicked breathing. Just then a crash of thunder rocked the cave again and Asher thought he felt some vibration under him.

Asher was completely overwhelmed with the feeling that he needed to get out of that cave, now. He quickly swept the dim flashlight beam in a 180-degree arc to get his bearings. He immediately determined the direction he came from and, head down, began his retreat from the cave with as much speed that he dared.

He splashed through the water and stumbled over stones. He was soaked to the waist as he trudged clumsily downstream in his desperate quest for the cave entrance. The thunder cracked again, this time with a deafening echo and Asher was sure that he had felt the ground shake under his feet.

Asher knew thunder and lightning did not shake the ground and that earthquakes did not make the thundering sounds like he had been hearing, but he could not think about that right now. He had to get out. He had to get out now.

He blew by his backpack, and shovel, and pickaxe, paying them no attention as he blundered through the twilight of the fading flashlight beam. Tink... tink... tink... The metal-on-stone din rang in his ears now. It was not in the distance. It was beside him, on top of him, under him, in the walls, in the ceiling, in the floor, in his ears, in his head. Tink...tink...tink...

He was moving faster and faster down the creek bed. And then he tripped, and then he fell fast, and then he landed hard. His left toes had caught an unseen protruding stone as he swung his foot forward to hop to the next stepping stone. He had landed mostly in the water catching himself with both hands as he threw his arms out in front of him.

As his right hand connected with a sharp rock, he released the flashlight. The flashlight flew from his grasp, hit another rock, shattered into pieces of red and chromed plastic, and then tumbled into the water. His light was gone for good.

He slowly picked himself up out of the water and stood there for a moment as the west branch of Old Indian Creek washed over his aching feet. He felt blood run down to his fingertips from a cut on his knuckles as his hand throbbed with pain. He was soaked from head to toe. Everything he had brought with him into the cave was gone now.

Asher was not sure which way was out as he stood there disoriented from the fall and in complete darkness. He breathed hard as he stood there, from the fall but also from the fright. He wanted to feel sorry for himself but the cave did not afford him the time to.

At that moment a new rumbling roar rose up behind him accompanied by the sound of falling rock and sand. Instinctively, Asher tried to rush in the opposite direction of the terrifying noise. He dropped to his hands and knees as there was no other way to navigate the terrain in the blackness. He heard more rumbling and more debris falling behind him.

Asher scrambled through the water and over the rocks like a terrified crab on the beach seeking shelter from a hungry gull. The crashing sound of the rocks and sand raining down behind him was getting louder, and so, getting closer. Asher was almost hysterical with the fear that the cave was going to collapse on him as he thrashed forward.

Finally, he saw it. The faint glow of daylight from the cave entrance. There was another deafening crash behind him. He popped up from his crawl and began running toward the light. With every step he was greeted with more and more daylight until he reached the cave's opening.

He did not look back or hesitate. He threw his body, head first into the jagged teeth of the opening. With both of his arms out in front of him, he ignored the pain in his cut and bruised hand and pulled as hard as he could to drag the rest of his body out of the cave. If there would have been someone there to see Asher exit from the cave, they would have said it looked like the mountain coughed him out.

He tumbled in a heap, landing mostly in the water and lay there as one final thunderous crash bellowed from the cave. It shook the ground violently as dust poured out of the caves entrance and rained down on Asher. Then it was silent. Only a crow cawed once in some distant tree.

Chapter 20

Exodus

Asher raised his head from the muddy creek side, blinking the water and sand out of his eyes. As his eyes came into focus, his gaze settled on what used to be the opening in the side of the mountain. There was a debris filled gap where the jagged mouth of the cave once was. The cave was gone, or at the very least, collapsed so re-entry was impossible. Asher closed his eyes and let his head fall back into the mud.

A feeling of relief, and at the same time, regret, washed over him as he lay in the muck beside Old Indian Creek. He was bleeding from his head and hand and likely other places too. His body throbbed with pain as the creek trickled beside him, and around him, and over him. So much gold, gone, but at least he was alive.

He opened his eyes again, still lying crumpled on his side, his cheek making a depression in the ground as pebbles and pine needles made depressions in his cheek. The sweet earthy smell of the creek-side filled his nostrils and replaced the decayed odor that had leached into him from that cave.

He lay there in a haze of exhaustion, trying to comprehend what had just happened.

"Was it an earthquake?" Asher asked himself knowing it was not.

"There's not a lot of earthquakes up in these parts," Claudie's words now echoed in Asher's head.

The cave was collapsed, and cursed, and haunted, and Asher's great grandfather's grave; and almost Asher's grave. The fact that the cave was full of gold now seemed completely irrelevant.

He raised his head once more and then slowly and deliberately raised the rest of his body from the creek side. He stood unsteadily with the storm clouds breaking overhead and giving way to brilliant sunshine. The clean after-storm-air breezed over his face as he squinted in the late afternoon sun's rays.

His saturated and tattered tee shirt began to dry along with the blood on his hand and forehead. Everything he had brought with him was buried in the cave. His backpack and everything in it, the pickaxe, the shovel, the flashlight, and the desire for him to find gold, had all been lost in the cave.

Asher took stock of his situation. He had lost most all of his camping gear to the collapse. He reached into his pockets to determine what, if anything, was left in them that could help him. He pulled out his compass and discovered it was shattered and useless. Beyond his compass, in the same pocket, Asher found the two nuggets he had put in there earlier.

He momentarily was excited that he had not lost the gold nuggets, then realized they would be of little use to get him back to the old barn before dark. In his other pocket he retrieved his Case pocketknife which he was thrilled to have not lost. He fished around in his back pockets hoping to find his lighter that he had put there that morning. He had no luck in the left pocket but success in the right.

He held the lighter in his right hand and flicked it once, twice and then the third time it sparked but did not light. It had gotten too wet for the flame to light. Asher really hoped it would dry out by nightfall. He would need a fire to dry out the clothes he was wearing, which were now the only clothes he had left. He returned the lighter to his front pocket before pivoting to survey the woods around him.

The fear that had gripped him in the cave was dissolving into a determined urgency. Asher needed to get to the old barn before nightfall and he estimated he had about one and a half hours to accomplish the hike. It was more than enough time if he still had a working compass, and something to eat, and dry clothes, and was not bruised and cut up from head to toe. He pushed the lost gold and the cave collapse to the back of his mind and summoned up his survival instincts.

"I can't spend the night in the open woods without a tent. This just cannot happen," Asher whispered allowed to himself with a panicked determination.

Asher knew his best bet would be to follow Old Indian Creek to the fork, cross to the east side, then try to determine an east by southeast heading to find the old barn. He was hopeful that he would recognize some land marks once he started through the woods away from the creek. He would not take any shortcuts. Asher could not afford any wrong turns this late in the day.

He gave the remnants of the cave entrance one last look as he watched Old Indian Creek bubble out from the side of the mountain like tears from a giant face. The entrance of the cave was completely plugged, but miraculously the creek continued to flow from the ground, gushing from the side of the mountain, just as it had for millennia.

The scent of burning pine swirled around Asher, wrapping around him like a well-worn blanket. He sat on the smooth field stone, stripped to his underwear, warming his aching body. His clothes hung on a nearby white birch sapling, steam wafting up in wisps as they dried from the warmth of the fire.

Asher had made it back to the old homestead without incident. He had followed the west branch of Old

Indian Creek to where it branched, and then used the setting sun to determine his bearing of east by southeast. It had not been long before Asher had recognized some landmarks to confirm he was on the right path.

He had arrived back at the old barn just in time to see the late August sun set in brilliant shades of pink, and purple, and crimson, promising a beautiful summer day to come. His lighter had dried out and he had quickly lit a fire with some shreds of birch bark that he had peeled off the nearby tree. Birch bark burns better than paper when used to start a fire. Asher was always amazed how the bark popped and sparked and burned so intensely, like it had been created to start fires.

The camp fire blazed with dead pine branches snapped from the base of surrounding trees as it warmed Asher's weary body. He sat almost too close letting the fire illuminate his face and heat his cheeks to a red hue. He was mesmerized, almost hypnotized, by the dancing flames as he contemplated the day's events.

Asher had gotten over the shock of finding the mother-load and then losing it. On the long hike back to the old barn he had realized that he had been lucky to escape the collapsed cave with his life. He had two gold nuggets more than he had started the day with, and that would just have to be enough.

Finding that skeleton put everything in perspective for Asher. He was sure that the remains he had found must have been his Great Grandpa Ansylum, if what Claudie had told him was true. Disturbing his grandfather's grave left Asher with more than a little feeling of regret. But still, all of that gold...

"Was the cave haunted by Ansylum's ghost?" That is the question that gnawed at Asher as he had hiked back to the old barn, and now, as he sat safely by the campfire.

Asher was not sure if he believed in hauntings or ghosts. He had never experienced anything that would suggest the existence of anything like that... until today.

What happened in that cave today was not natural, was not explainable, was not believable.

Unless someone had seen it with their own eyes and heard it with their own ears, they would not believe it. Asher could barely believe it himself and he had just lived through it. It seemed almost like a dream, or more accurately, a nightmare to Asher already. He closed his eyes to conger the eerie metal on stone tink… tink… The sound clanged in his ears with vivid recollection and Asher knew he had not dreamed it.

He could not tell anyone about his adventure. No one would believe him. Given his failure to collect any quantity of gold, Asher did not think he wanted to tell anyone anyways.

"You're only a hero if you get the treasure in the end, not just survive," thought Asher with a disappointed sigh.

Asher bunched the coals from the fire into the center of the fire pit so they could safely burn themselves out. He retrieved his clothes from the birch tree and dressed his bruised body. He had already eaten what was left of the peanut butter and jam sandwiches and there was nothing left to do but try to get some sleep.

He scaled the supporting pole once more to the loft of the falling down barn. He was very happy that he had decided to leave his sleeping bag behind with the jar of gold dust wrapped safely in it. He unrolled it directly in the middle of the floor of the loft exposing the jar of gold he had stowed there. With some effort, he managed to unscrew the lid from the old jar and then dropped the two gold nuggets in with the gold dust.

He shook the jar a little as he peered in at the gold, trying to get the faint starlight to reflect in the yellow hue.

"It could have gone worse," Asher supposed, as he replaced the lid of the blackened jar.

His body ached for sleep as he slipped into his dew dampened sleeping bag and zipped himself in tight against the cool night air. The crickets and frogs chirped their endless nighttime songs, lulling Asher quickly into dream land.

That night Asher dreamed that he was drowning in a golden sea. He had dreamed that he was caught by an undertow that struggled to pull him under. Uncle Jeb had dragged him to safety at the last moment, depositing him on a beach made of gold dust. Uncle Jeb had then sunk back beneath the golden waves and disappeared after he had saved Asher from certain death.

Asher awoke with a start. A feeling of loss lingered with him long after he had awakened from his dream. In the early morning twilight, Asher had a strong desire to see his Uncle Jeb. Luckily, that is exactly where he was headed today.

Chapter 21

Loss

As he blinked the sleep from his eyes he thought about the trek back to Uncle Jeb's cabin today. He wished he was returning with a fortune in gold. At least he was returning with no broken bones and, well, not dead. Asher crawled out of his sleeping bag as the sun rose and a new day began.

He rolled the jar of gold into the center of his sleeping bag and tied it tight with fishing line from his fishing reel. With no backpack or rope, he needed a way to carry the awkward bundle. He took the thick cords that were meant to tie up the sleeping bag and knotted them into two loops. Then he awkwardly slipped the loops over his shoulders so the sleeping bag rested on his back. The cords cut in a little, but it would have to do.

He had already wedged his fishing pole into the folds of his sleeping bag before slinging it up on his back. He gave the old homestead one more look and then started down what used to be the old homestead driveway. The morning sun burned bright as he reached the field stone wall. The last wisps of the morning fog burned off in the sunlight and gave way to a brilliant blue and green late summer morning. The air was fresh after yesterday's storm without a hint of humidity.

Asher would arrive at Uncle Jeb's cabin a whole day earlier than he had originally planned. It was only

Saturday morning, though to Asher, it felt like he had been gone a week. Uncle Jeb surely would not mind. He would be glad to see Asher. He would be happy to see that Asher was safe and sound.

Asher marched on, along the sinking rock wall and into the woods until the line of stones all but disappeared. He emerged out of the woods at the far end of the swamp, closest to Uncle Jeb's cabin. It was still very early this brilliant summer morning. The sun hovered just above the tree line burning intensely like the fabled Alexandria Lighthouse.

As Asher approached the Barker posted signs he did not even hesitate. He knew the brothers would never be up yet. Early rising was in the same class as manual labor for the Barker brothers, they just did not do it. Asher never broke stride as he descended the hill and entered the disputed strip of land. He hiked straight across, feeling pretty smug about being up and about before the brothers were out of bed.

Asher had been right. The brothers were not there to bother him. In fact, the only sound he heard in the woods was a lone woodpecker hammering away at a stub of an elm tree, its sharp beak drilling for breakfast. He crossed the second line of posted signs and strode confidently up to the crest of the hill.

As Asher started down the next side of the hill, he mulled over how much he should tell Uncle Jeb about his adventure in the cave. Maybe he should not tell him anything about what had happened yesterday. After all it would be admitting that he had went exactly where Uncle Jeb had warned him not to. No, maybe best not to tell him anything about the cave or the gold.

Asher would have to come up with some sort of story to tell his uncle. He had lost almost everything he had brought with him. Uncle Jeb was old, but he was still sharp, and not much got by him. He would surely realize Asher had returned without his gear.

As Asher hiked along Old Indian Creek he tried out different stories and excuses in his head that he might be able to tell Uncle Jeb. Not one of the scenarios seemed plausible. What to tell his uncle? Maybe he would have to tell the truth. After all, the truth was not all that believable either.

His thoughts were abruptly interrupted when he glanced up from the creek bed and spied his uncle's cabin. Asher was ecstatic to see the worn structure and broke into a trot as he approached. After his ordeal out in the woods, he wanted to see Uncle Jeb rocking in his chair, pipe smoke drifting into the log rafters of the old porch. He could not wait to sit and sip on a cold grape soda. He even wanted to hear the eerie creek of the rocking chair that so unsettled him. He wanted the comfort of the familiar.

Asher jogged up to the south end of the cabin then rounded the corner to face the porch. The rocking chair was empty. Uncle Jeb was always up at the crack of dawn. He would have already eaten his two eggs and two pieces of toast for breakfast by now. He would have filled his bird feeder with bird seed and his pipe with Amish pipe tobacco. He would have been sitting in his rocking chair, rocking, smoking, and watching his birds. But, he was not, he had not. Where was he?

"Uncle Jeb," Asher called out as he started up the well-worn porch steps. "Uncle Jeb, where are you?"

Asher felt his chest tighten when he did not receive an answer.

"Uncle Jeb! I'm back early!" Asher called out louder.

There was no answer. Impossibly, there was no answer. Uncle Jeb never left the vicinity of the cabin. Asher's parents even brought him his groceries. He just did not ever leave. Where could he be?

"Uncle Jeb, where are you? It's Asher. I'm back early," Asher called out again, this time with more desperation then he had intended.

The feeling in Asher's chest tightened like a vise, and migrated to the base of his throat. He felt his heart begin to throb and pound in the center of his chest, and in his head, and in his ears.

"Uncle Jeb, where are you?" By now he was shouting. He knew there was something wrong.

Asher grasped the busted handle on the ancient screen door. The door served as the summer entry door to the cabin, barely keeping insects out and not quite latching into place. It creaked open with a deafening screech.

"Uncle Jeb?" Asher inquired in a lowered tone as he entered the cabin.

His Uncle's bed was in the far north corner of the one room cabin. Asher was suddenly aware that Uncle Jeb had not gotten up yet.

"He must be sick." Asher thought to himself as he regretted all of his earlier yelling. "He must be sleeping in. He must be trying to sleep off whatever ailment he has," Asher reasoned.

Asher crept into the cabin and drew closer to Uncle Jeb. He wanted to see if he indeed was still sleeping. If he was not, maybe Asher could get something for him, maybe he could do something for him. The tightness in Asher's chest, the lump in his throat, the shallow breathing, it was all still there as he moved across the cabin floor toward the simple single bed.

Asher crouched at the edge of the bed, peering closely at his sleeping uncle. Only Uncle Jeb was not breathing. His body did not move at all. Asher studied his uncle's chest that was partially covered by a hundred-year-old patchwork quilt, trying to discern some movement. Trying to see a rise or a fall or any movement, but there was nothing.

Asher stood for a long moment, watching, and not being able to breath himself. He finally reached out a trembling hand and just barely touched Uncle Jeb's weathered cheek with his fingertips. His cheek was cold.

By now, Asher had expected that, but it still did not prepare him for it.

"Dead…" The thought, the realization, the finality, the awful truth. It hit Asher square in the chest like an expertly swung baseball bat and he fell to his knees as he absorbed the blow.

"No, no, no, no, no, no…!" Asher's chant started in a whisper and ended in screaming rage. "You can't be dead. You can't be dead!" The tears streamed from Asher's eyes as he screeched into the empty cabin.

Asher finally fell silent as he knelt by Uncle Jeb's bed, trying to swallow the golf ball lump that had lodged in the back of his throat, and blink back the tears that insisted on flowing so freely from his reddened eyes. He breathed in deeply, and then slowly let the breath out through pursed lips. What should his next move be? Asher, for the first time in his life, was at a loss for what to do next.

He stood slowly, not taking his eyes off from his uncle. Uncle Jeb did look peaceful, like he was sleeping, like he might suddenly open his eyes and sit up, but his color was wrong. Uncle Jeb's color in his face was not of this world, not of the living. Asher turned away. He could not bear to look at him any longer.

Chapter 22

Treasure

Asher walked around the one room cabin as he thought about Uncle Jeb lying there, not moving, not breathing, not living. What should he do next? Just then Asher noticed an open notebook on the handmade pine dresser next to the single bed. Asher crossed the worn wide plank floor to the dresser to investigate the open book.

It was one of those old style lined notebooks with the mottled black and white cardboard cover, bound with canvas tape and string rather than wire spiral bound. It lay open to roughly the center of the book and had a look of years and wear.

He read the heading on the notebook paper. It was written in a beautiful stylized cursive script, even if a bit shaky. The heading on the notebook paper read *My Last Will and Testament*. Asher's breath caught in his throat.

"He knew..." Asher whispered in a gasp at the sudden realization of what the opened notebook meant.

"He knew before he went to bed last night. Did he know before that? Did he know when he saw me last?" The questions churned in Asher's mind and stomach.

Asher grasped the notebook, holding it in both hands with the reverence it deserved. He carried it slowly over to the to the ancient slab-style kitchen table that had been cut from a single old growth white pine before his Great Grandpa Ansylum was born. He sat on the massive bench that had been cut from the same tree, and gently placed the notebook, still open, on the table before him. The natural light from the nine light panel window spilled over the immense kitchen table and onto the waiting notebook.

Asher struggled to read the stylized script before him.

To my grandnephew, Asher Mason, I leave my hunting coat and my hunting knife. To my nephew and niece, Eleanor and Mike Asher, I leave all of my land and the rest of my worldly possessions including my cabin.

Asher read the script once more. Uncle Jeb had left everything to Asher's parents, which was not a surprise, after all, they were Uncle Jeb's closest relatives. Everything but his hunting jacket and hunting knife was left to Asher's parents. Asher could not believe that he was specifically named in Uncle Jeb's will.

The writing was stylized and jittery but unmistakable. Uncle Jeb wanted Asher to have his hunting coat and hunting knife. This struck Asher as a strange selection for him but who was he to question his uncle's gift. He could not believe that Uncle Jeb had named him at all.

He rose from the massive kitchen table and moved to the coat tree that stood by the entry door like a sentry guarding the haven that was Uncle Jeb's cabin. The coat tree actually was a real tree. It was a young cherry tree cut from the front yard and nailed to a pine board base. Its branches poked out from all directions creating countless places to hang coats or anything else you might want to.

Uncle Jeb's green plaid Woolrich hunting jacket hung on the cherry coat tree, eclipsing everything else that hung there. Asher grasped the jacket with both hands and lifted it off its perch and held it in front of him. He brought it close to his face and breathed deeply. It smelled of pipe tobacco, and leather, and days gone by, and Uncle Jeb. It was almost more than Asher could stand.

Asher slipped the old hunting jacket over one arm, then the other, and then he was wearing it. It fit him perfectly. How did that happen? How did Asher become the same size of his beloved Uncle that was so much larger than him? He buttoned the hunting jacket up to his chin, despite the heat of the summer morning.

Asher raised his arms and then dropped them to his side, trying out his new coat that was older than he was. He exited the cabin to the porch and stood there motionless and silent, thinking. Uncle Jeb's rocking chair sat before him, beckoning him to sit and rock. He stared at the creepy family heirloom, wishing it was not calling to him to take Uncle Jeb's place.

Asher lowered himself into the ancient chair. As he sat in the Mason rocking chair, Asher felt a comfortable familiarity, like he had been sitting there his whole life, like maybe he would die in that chair.

Uncle Jeb's hunting coat wrapped Asher in a comfortable embrace as he sat and rocked. Creak... creak... creak... The creaking sound that so unsettled Asher just days ago, now comforted him. Dead... Uncle Jeb is dead. Asher just could not wrap his brain around it.

Asher knew he needed to call someone. He knew he needed to tell someone so they could do what needed to be done. So someone could do the next thing, whatever that was. Asher shoved his hands in the pockets of the sacred hunting jacket and rocked hard as tears flowed down his cheeks. The creak of the chair bellowed in his ears and there was nothing else in the world but the Mason rocking chair, rocking furiously on the hallowed porch of his ancestors.

Asher was suddenly aware of something in the pocket of the hunting jacket. He stopped rocking. His left hand closed around a small piece of paper that he pulled from the scratchy wool pocket. The yellowed paper was folded into a neat square with crisp folded edges and Asher's name was clearly written across the front of it. Asher held it between his thumb and forefinger just inches from his face scrutinizing the unlikely folded paper.

Asher unfolded the square of paper until it was an open sheet that splayed across his hands. The words were faint and Asher could barely make out the penciled scrawl.

Dear Asher,

Apparently I'm dead, so my fortune is yours. Thank you for your companionship and friendship. I've spent the last forty years panning for gold on The Old Indian Creek. The treasure I left behind is the result of that. I've stowed it under the chest of drawers, hidden below the floor boards. I ask that you keep the fortune a secret. Use what you need to keep the land in the Mason family. Otherwise, do what you want with it. I have left a contact number of a trusted gold dealer from out of state that will help you convert the gold to cash. Goodbye Asher.

Love, Uncle Jeb

Asher stared at the note that had been left just for him in the pocket of the hunting jacket. He read it again, and then another time. Salty tears streaked down Asher's flushed cheeks and found his quivering lips. Asher's mind raced. He needed to call an adult to tell them about Uncle Jeb. But he needed to investigate what was under the chest of drawers before he made that call.

He once again smelled the Amish brand pipe tobacco as he wiped the tears from his face with the sleeve of Uncle Jeb's scratchy wool coat. He breathed in deeply, held his breath for a moment, then slowly sighed out a long breath through pursed lips. If he was going to keep Uncle Jeb's treasure a secret, he needed to calm down and focus. First he had to find the treasure.

He crossed the wide plank floor to the heavy homemade chest of drawers. The solid pine chest was as tall as him, it held five huge drawers, and probably weighed three hundred pounds. How was he going to move this? Asher stood beside it, sizing the huge piece of furniture up. He thought maybe he could just shove it out of the way enough to get to the floor beneath.

He bent down and hugged the massive piece of furniture in its middle, planted his feet on the plank floor, and heaved hard. It did not move, not even a little. He shifted his position slightly, braced his feet again and heaved with everything he had. The chest of drawers moved an inch.

Asher relaxed his body to prepare for another all-out shove. As he paused, still leaning on the chest, he noticed that the chest left gouge marks in the planks of the floor where it had slid. This was not going to work. If he left gouges in the floor the full width of the chest of drawers, anyone that walked in the cabin would surely notice it had been moved recently. He needed a new plan.

Asher stood and surveyed the cabin as he thought about his predicament. Uncle Jeb had to be able to get under that chest once in a while. How did he do it? He inspected the floor by his feet to see if there were any scratches in the planks from moving the chest. There were no scratches but there were slight lines scuffed in the floor, as if something much softer than a piece of furniture had been dragged there.

"He put something under it to slide it on," Asher murmured with sudden realization.

He scanned the room again. His eyes rested on just the perfect thing to put under the chest of drawers. Laying on the floor in front of the screechy old screen door was a large oval rag mat. It was called a rag mat because it was made from strips of rags that had been hand crocheted into a flat, rough door mat. It had been made by Asher's great grandmother during a particularly long and harsh

Adirondack winter. The mat's bright patchwork of colors had long since faded and now was dyed by the dirt to a dull brown.

"Perfect!" Asher whispered excitedly.

He hauled the mat out to the porch and held it over the wobbly railing. He shook it furiously, then banged it on the railing, trying to get it to release its years of sand and dirt. A great cloud of dust bellowed from the rug. When Asher was satisfied that he had pounded all he could out of the rug, he dragged it back into the cabin and across the floor to the chest of drawers.

He placed the rug next to the base then leaned hard on the very top of the drawers. I tipped surprisingly easy and Asher thought that it must be top heavy. When one side of the base of the drawers rocked off the floor, Asher shoved a corner of the rug under it a few inches. He repeated the motion three more times until the rug was under most of the base.

Again Asher bent down and hugged the set of drawers and then heaved as hard as he could. This time the chest slid fairly easy, moving it a whole foot to the side. He shoved again and again until the entire floor space where the chest of drawers stood was exposed. And now he inspected the thick pine floor boards for a trap door.

At first he did not see it. He ran his hands along the seams of the planks pushing and pulling at them. He rapped his knuckles on the floor boards, starting at the far left corner, and working his way toward him. It sounded solid, and solid, and solid, and hollow…

"There it is," Asher whispered.

Asher looked closer at the hollow sounding spot in the floor. He could just make out a crossway seam that fit so perfectly it had looked like a continuous board. He pulled his jackknife out of his pocket and locked out the blade. Wedging the tip of the blade in the seam between the planks next to the crossway seam, he gently worked it in about a half an inch. He jiggled and twisted the knife as the plank eased up and out of its comfortable resting place.

With both hands he pulled on the tight fitting pine plank and it came free with a "thunk." Asher peered in the dark space below the floor board, straining to make out the objects within. In three neat rows sat twelve jars, four in each. Asher reached down, kneeling beside the small cavity in the floor, and grasped a jar. He raised it up and out to the light. It was a jar of pickles.

"Pickles? Really?" Asher said aloud annoyed and exasperated.

Asher set the jar beside him on the floor as his mind sputtered with the unlikely jar-of-pickles theme of the last few days. He pulled out another jar. It was another jar of pickled cucumbers. He held the jar close to his face as he scrutinized it. Maybe there was gold dust hidden among the cucumbers, and garlic, and stems of dill. He wondered if vinegar reacted with gold. He turned the jar slowly around, tipping it this way and that, until he was satisfied there was no gold among the pickles.

He set the jar down beside the first and worked to retrieve the remaining ten jars. They were all full of dill pickles. There was no gold.

"Maybe Uncle Jeb hid some gold dust inside the individual pickles," Asher thought to himself, knowing that he was grasping at straws now.

He reached back down into the cavity in the floor, plunging his arm to past his elbow and felt around the bottom. As he did, the board that made up the floor of the space moved a little. His fingers searched and probed along the edges until he found what he was looking for. It was a small hole just big enough for one finger.

He shoved his index finger into the little hole and pulled. The false bottom lifted and a piece of lumber that was a little smaller than the dimensions of the space pulled free. Under the rectangular piece of lumber were three more rows of canning jars. There were another twelve jars in total. Asher grasped a jar and lifted it out of its hiding place into the daylight.

It was a pint size Mason jar that was filled half way with gold dust. He set it on the floor next to him, pulled another jar out, and sat it beside the first. It was the same size jar, but this one was full. Asher's mouth gaped as he stared at Uncle Jeb's secret. He blinked twice, barely breathing, and then retrieved the next jar. It was full too. He plunked it down beside the other jars.

Asher retrieved the remainder of the dozen jars, on at a time, one after the other, until they all sat side by side in a neat row. The rest of the jars were also full of gold dust.

"Uncle Jeb was a millionaire!" He was a multimillionaire…" Asher said aloud shocked and somewhat confused. "But he lived like he was penniless."

Asher knelt there on the floor in front of the millions of dollars worth of gold, staring at the line of shimmering jars, blinking slowly once in a while. He expected the glittering jars to disappear after he had opened his eyes from one of the exaggerated blinks. But there they were, lined up in front of him, like a dozen golden glowing beacons emitting their own light. Impossibly, there they were.

The screen door clapped suddenly and Asher whipped his head around to see who had come in. His heart was in his throat with the sudden realization that someone was about to find out Uncle Jeb's secret, that was now Asher's secret. The screen door clapped again, but there was no one there. It had only been a gust of wind playing with the unlatched screen door. It banged again and then settled back in its well-worn resting position. Asher exhaled a sigh and then began breathing again.

He was more than a little relieved that it had been just the wind, but the unexpected gust was a little unsettling. It had been a deathly still day up until that moment. The banging screen door was also a reminder to

Asher that he needed to figure out his next move before someone really did show up.

Asher decided that he would take two of the jars home with him and leave the rest in the secret floor space. He figured that the gold would be safer there than any place Asher could find to hide it. He worked feverously to replace the jars of gold to where he had found them. Then he replaced the false bottom and then finally put the jars of dill pickles back in their original resting place.

He replaced the floor board, with some effort, pounding it back into place with the heel of his hand. He carefully slid the hulking pine chest of drawers back to the exact spot it had sat for decades. Its original position of the chest was marked by the sun darkened wood around it, like a chalk outline from a murder scene.

He tipped the chest of drawers and yanked the hand crocheted rug out from under it, then returned the rug to threshold of the screen door. He surveyed the room, making certain everything looked as it did when he had first arrived that morning. Everything looked as it should.

Asher had kept one full jar of gold and the one that was half full out to take home with him. Now he picked the jars up and cradled one in each arm. Asher noticed something other than gold dust in the jar only half full. He set the full jar on the massive pine plank table, then unscrewed the lid to the half full jar.

A tiny scrap of paper lay mostly on top of the gold dust, its corner buried just a little. Asher reached in the jar and retrieved the slip of paper. It had a name and a ten-digit phone number carefully printed on it. It was the contact number of the trusted out of state gold dealer. Asher smiled with satisfaction at the discovery of the name and number.

Asher strode out of the cabin and onto the porch to where he had tossed his sleeping bag. He cut the fishing line that bound it, and then rolled it out onto the weathered porch floor. He removed the jar that he had rolled up in it. He paused for a moment to gaze at the gold dust and two gold nuggets he had found on his adventure. Then he unscrewed the lids to the partially full jars and combined the contents.

Asher placed the two gold filled jars on the foot of his sleeping bag and then rolled them up securely into the center where they could not be seen. He placed his sleeping bag on the cabin porch next to the screen door.

"Time to make the call," Asher announced to himself.

He entered the cabin and crossed the wide pine plank floor to where an antique phone clung to the wall. The phone was a putrid green color, but worst of all, it was an old fashion rotary dial. Asher hated using it in the best of circumstances, and this was the worst of circumstances.

He placed his index finger in the three hole of the rotary dial, spun it around to the metal stop, and then released it. The rotary dial made its weird noise as it returned to where it had started from. Asher repeated the motion with the four hole and then with the rest of the seven-digit phone number. He breathed in deep, then breathed out slow in a long exhale as he prepared himself for the conversation.

"Hi, Mom? It's Asher. Um… Something's happened to Uncle Jeb," Asher began.

"Um… No he's not alright," Asher answered his mother.

"He's… um… well… he passed away last night," Asher finally got the words out.

"Yea. I'm fine," He reassured his mother.

"Last night, in his sleep I guess. I found him this morning in his bed," Asher informed her.

"Okay, I'll wait for you to get here. No, I'm fine. I'll see you soon," Asher hung the antique phone receiver back onto its perch after saying goodbye to his nearly hysterical mother.

There was nothing else to do but wait. His mind and stomach churned with conflicting emotions as he thought about his beloved Uncle Jeb dead in the cabin and the mountain of gold that his uncle had left to him. He sat in the Mason family rocking chair with Uncle Jeb's wool hunting coat wrapped around him, staring out at Old Indian Creek, trying to make sense of it all. Creak... creak... creak...

Epilogue

Asher jogged down Main Street as brightly colored maple leaves floated down around him, falling to the ground like the first light snowfall of winter. He panted and pumped his arms to the rhythm of his stride. Asher glanced over his shoulder as he passed her driveway. Adeline strode up from behind him and quickly matched his pace.

"Mind if I join you?" Adeline asked

"No. Um… definitely," Asher answered with too much enthusiasm and not enough confidence.

"Nice Nikes," Adeline complemented.

"Thanks," Asher said with too much satisfaction as he looked over at her and smiled.

96795538R00078

Made in the USA
Columbia, SC
06 June 2018